GOODBYE, GALACTICA!

They weren't even making any effort to escape! The *Galactica* might possibly be able to make it, but that would mean leaving the rest of the fleet to be destroyed and that fool Adama would never do that. They were going to stand and fight against overwhelming odds. They had no chance, none whatsoever. Baltar knew he would get his victory and his place in Cylon history would be assured . . .

"This is going to be a classic defeat," exulted Baltar, licking his lips. "It will be spoken of throughout the Cylon nation for the next thousand yahrens! Goodbye, *Galactica*. Goodbye, Adama!"

BattlestaR GALACTICA 6
THE LIVING LEGEND

Novel by
GLEN A. LARSON
AND NICHOLAS YERMAKOV
Based on the Universal Television Series
"BATTLESTAR GALACTICA"
Created by Glen A. Larson
Adapted from the episodes
"The Living Legend, Parts I and II"
Teleplay by Glen A. Larson
Story by Ken Pettus and Glen A. Larson

BERKLEY BOOKS, NEW YORK

BATTLESTAR GALACTICA 6:
THE LIVING LEGEND

A Berkley Book / published by arrangement with
MCA PUBLISHING, a Division of MCA Inc.

PRINTING HISTORY
Berkley edition / April 1982

ISBN: 0-425-05249-4

A BERKLEY BOOK ® TM 757,375
Berkley Books are published by Berkley Publishing Corporation,
200 Madison Avenue, New York, New York 10016.
The name "BERKLEY" and the stylized "B" with design are
trademarks belonging to Berkley Publishing Corporation.
PRINTED IN THE UNITED STATES OF AMERICA

PROLOGUE

Troy sat at the console in his cabin aboard the *Galactica*. He was alone and he stared at the screen, on which appeared the face of a very old man. The man was Troy's adoptive grandfather and, when he had been alive, he was the commander of the *Battlestar Galactica*.

"Troy," said Adama, "I know it's you because no one else will ever receive the key to this program. If you're viewing this then I must be dead. Perhaps, I have no way of knowing, I have only just passed on or perhaps I have been dead for a period of time. There's no telling what the future holds in store and I have no way of knowing when you will be hearing these words, much less if you will ever be hearing them. But if you are, then I know that the Lord has preserved you and that you are now the new commander of the *Galactica*."

The image of Adama paused.

"As I speak these words, I know that I am dying. It does not disturb me. I am prepared to die. I have lived a long and fruitful life and the Lord has seen fit to allow me to survive this long. I can ask for no more than that and I am content.

"If there was one thing I could have asked for which I have not received, it is that my son did not outlive me. I—I still feel his loss. When I think of all the yahrens that he served under me as my strike commander, the finest Viper pilot I have ever known, the bravest warrior, it pains me when I think that in all those yahrens I never once told him that I loved him. Oh, he knew I did, but it would have meant so much more, I know, had I been able to say those words out loud."

Adama's image sighed deeply. For a moment, Troy thought that he would not be able to continue, but then he spoke again.

"Your father was a great man, Troy. You were just a child when he died. Do you remember? We all used to call you 'Boxey.' I remember how you came to hate that name as you grew older and we had to find another for you, since we never knew your real one. But that's beside the point. Forgive an old man's rambling. I remember how you tried not to cry the day Apollo didn't come back from his mission. In a sense, you were wiser than I was that day, for you knew the truth, while I foolishly allowed myself to hope that some miracle would restore him to me once again, as had happened the last time he failed to return from a mission."

Adama paused again, thinking back.

"That was when we found Cain," he said. "Your father came back from the dead that day and brought another with him. He had been a good friend and I had thought him dead for over two yahrens. You were very young then, Troy and I don't know if you'll remember, but he saved all our lives.

"That is but one chapter in the history of the *Galactica*. I had hoped that her next commander after me would be my son, but that was not to be. The *Galactica* is yours now, Troy, and it is for you to decide her destiny. But before you determine the future of your ship, you should know her past.

"It's all here, in this program, the key to which no one has but you. These are my journals, Troy. I have kept them fastidiously ever since that day, back on Caprica, that the *Galactica* was commissioned and mine became her guiding hand. She has known no master but me in all those yahrens and now she passes on to you. No one else has ever seen my journals, Troy. You are the first. What you will do with them after you have seen them is up to you. Scan them in order, if you like, from the beginning to the end . . . or from the present point to the beginning . . . or according to your own memory. If there are incidents that you remember, the computer can locate those sections of the journals for you. All you need do is ask.

"My final words to you, Troy, are these: circumstances made it impossible for you to have anything even remotely resembling a normal childhood. For that, I am sorry, even though you've grown into a man that I respect. We tried our best to make a home for the children in the fleet, for they were our hope for the future, but in your case, it was very hard. You lost your real parents back when Caprica was destroyed. You gained a new father in Apollo and you came to love him, only to lose your father once again. You gained a new mother in Serena, only to lose your mother for a second time when Serena died. Twice orphaned, you became a very quiet child, so different from the way you once had been.

"I tried to be the best grandfather I knew how, but that was not enough. Having twice been orphaned, you put up barriers that no one could get through. You didn't want to love anyone ever again, for fear of losing them. It was a long time before anyone could break through to you. I have some knowledge of how you must have felt for I, too, had barriers of my own.

"You never really knew your father, Troy. Learn about him now. Learn about the man. It's all here, God knows, it's all that I have left. But before I leave you, there's one thing more I want to say. I almost said it to Apollo, that time with Cain, but I didn't and regret it to this day. I have since said it to you, but I want to say it once again.

"I love you. And farewell."

The screen went blank.

Troy sat for a long time in silence. Finally, he leaned forward to the console to begin Adama's journals.

He would start with Cain.

CHAPTER ONE

For the Viper fighter pilots of the *Battlestar Galactica*, there was no such thing as a routine patrol. Both Starbuck and Apollo knew that routine bred complacency. They could not afford to think of any of their scouting missions as "just another routine patrol," in spite of the countless missions that they flew, in spite of the sameness of many of those missions.

There had been a time, when both Starbuck and Apollo had first entered the cockpits of their Vipers as newly graduated cadets, when they had felt the keen thrill of anticipation that came to all newly commissioned officers embarking upon their maiden flights. Although all cadets had opportunities to solo prior to receiving their commissions, it was not the same as piloting a Viper fighter for the first time without each little action being observed and evaluated by an instructor. Back then, they had known that there would be no one waiting for them when they returned, if they returned, to either compliment them on their performance or to point out the mistakes they made. If there was to be a test, it would be administered by Cylon fighters. And there would be no opportunity to make up for a poor score.

Yet, even though their baptism of fire had not come with their first missions, the thrill of piloting their Vipers for the first time as officers of the fleet had not been diminished. It was only much later that they became aware of the dangers of routine.

As children, they had both dreamed of spaceflight, but as adults, they learned the sad reality that spaceflight was often boring. Once the novelty wore off, the fascination faded. To a seasoned Viper pilot, flying a scouting mission was as mundane as walking. Starbuck and Apollo piloted their Vipers as though the sleek machines were extensions of their bodies. They were able to perform most of their functions without thinking, automatically, much as it took no thought to put one foot before the other. But with the ever present danger of a Cylon fighter squadron appearing out of nowhere, there was no room for a pilot to relax into a comfortable feeling of routine. If such an attack came, there would be no time for hesitation. Expert pilots had been blasted to debris because they had allowed themselves to become distracted, lost in reverie on a "routine" mission. *Every* mission had to be flown as though they might encounter the enemy at any time, even if there was no reported

Cylon activity in the sector they patrolled. A Viper pilot had to remain constantly on the alert. Paranoia was a very useful quality in a warrior.

Still, functioning at a peak level of awareness was exhausting. Whenever a pilot began to feel the strain of maintaining a constant state of watchfulness, his mind began to wander. To prevent this, pilots kept up a steady stream of chatter amongst themselves whenever they flew patrols. It was a way of reaching out across the distance that separated their fighters, a way of staying alert, of having the comforting feeling that a friend was near to lend a hand if need be. The camaraderie that resulted from this seemingly idle chatter was something only a pilot could understand. After returning from a mission, then there would be time in which to unwind, time to relax with their launch crews, their friends, their fellow shipmates.

For Captain Apollo, if the patrol showed that the *Galactica* and its rag-tag fleet were in no imminent danger of attack from Cylon forces, there would be time to spend alone with his son, Boxey. If she could find time off from her duties, his sister would often join them, as well. Apollo cherished those private moments with Boxey and Athena. They were his family. Even though he had adopted Boxey, who had been orphaned when the colony on Caprica had been destroyed, Apollo loved the boy no less than he would have had the child been his own. His and Serena's.

There was a void within him that had been there since the day Serena died. There were ways for Apollo to avoid that gut-wrenching feeling of despair whenever he thought of life without her. In the heat of battle, he never felt the loss. Sometimes he used his duties aboard the *Galactica* as a shield to protect himself from feeling the pain, but all efforts at escaping his grief were, at best, temporary solutions. He told himself that, with time, the pain would diminish. But no one knew just how much time they had.

The war had brought the two of them together and the war had torn them apart. Their time together had been so unendurably short.... Whenever he thought of Serena, Apollo's vision would begin to blur with barely restrained tears. He could not permit himself to cry while on a mission, or in view of his shipmates. But sometimes, in his private quarters, the nightmare visions of Caprica burning would awaken him and, instinctively, he would reach out for Serena. And she would not be there. Then, where no one else could see or hear him, Apollo would permit himself to grieve. He wept for the loss of his wife, for the loss of Caprica and the other colony worlds, and for the loss of the close relationship he once had with his father.

Apollo loved Adama and he knew that his father loved him, but they could never go back to the way things once had been, before Apollo won his commission, before the Cylon treachery that made them all orphans of the stars. The bond between father and son was there, as was the love, but the war meant that before Adama was his father, he was his commander. That placed an often painful, but necessary distance between them.

Adama bore the awesome burden of responsibility for the survivors of the holocaust. Their welfare, their survival, came first. If that meant sending his son out to die, Adama would do it. It was his duty, as it was Apollo's to lay down his life, if necessary, to protect the fleet. It was something both father and son understood. Both of them accepted it. They had no choice.

Starbuck, on the other hand, had his own ways of spending his time alone following a mission, of dealing with the pressure of their situation. In a way, it was not as hard for

Starbuck as it was for Apollo, because Starbuck thrived on pressure. And Starbuck thrived on war. That was the most difficult thing for him to deal with. Starbuck was not a war lover. There was insanity in that. He despised the war with the Cylons with a fury unmatched by anyone's save, perhaps, Apollo's. Yet Starbuck was a warrior. He knew that it was what he had been born to be. During his off-duty hours, he liked to pass his time playing cards and drinking baharri with the other pilots; he enjoyed the company of women and they, in turn, liked him. But Starbuck knew that the only time he ever really came alive was when he was in the cockpit of his Viper, engaging Cylon fighters in the biggest gamble of them all, the deadly game of life and death.

Like Apollo, Starbuck had been born during the war. He had never known anything else, none of the survivors had. It seemed to him that the human race had been at war with the Cylons since the dawn of time, fighting for their lives against an enemy dedicated to the total annihilation of the human race. He longed for peace. In spite of that, Starbuck often wondered if there would be a place for him in a time of peace. He was a warrior, a maverick, a gambler. In his quiet, private moments, he wrestled with the dilemma of his own existence. He wondered what it was about him that filled him with such vibrant vitality each time he entered combat. What was it that led him to take chances no one else would take? What strange, perverse aspect of his personality drove him to gamble with the Reaper, often taking foolhardy risks, just so he could revel in the thrill of beating Death? When sleep would not come, Starbuck would lie in his bunk, staring at the ceiling, wondering what sort of man lived for the risk of dying. He did not know the answer, and sometimes he wasn't sure he wished to know. It was a side of him that no one knew about. To the crew of the *Galactica*, Lieutenant Starbuck was a carefree rogue, a highly skilled pilot, an inveterate gambler, a womanizer and a rake. The old military catchphrase "Never volunteer for anything" had become known to the men and women of the *Galactica* as "Starbuck's Law." Yet those who knew him well, especially those who served with him, knew that in spite of his reputation for selfishness and self-preservation, Starbuck somehow always wound up flying those missions that, as he would put it, no one else would take on a bet.

It was a hard life. A life that had to be lived entirely for the present. They could allow themselves to have hopes for the future, but as warriors they had to live one centon at a time. They had to fly their missions with their eyes glued to their instruments, never allowing their attention to wander. To the younger men and women in the rag-tag fleet, especially the cadets, the life of a fighter pilot seemed glamorous, full of adventure. Starbuck and Apollo, both seasoned veterans of the war, knew better. War had no glamour. And the taste of adventure soured rapidly when the adrenaline rush that came with combat wore off and the profound exhaustion set in, the exhaustion and the shakes which every pilot experienced, but none would admit to, even to each other.

Sitting in the cockpit of his Viper, Apollo handled the controls with an ease that came only after yahrens of steady practice. His gaze never left the scanner. He was locked into a mode of hair-trigger awareness and it felt good to know that Starbuck's Viper paced him. The two men functioned together like a well-oiled machine. Despite the differences in their personalities, as Viper pilots they complemented each other perfectly.

They were nearing the return point of what had been an

uneventful scouting patrol when something made the hairs at the base of Apollo's neck bristle. He shivered slightly, as if he had just felt something crawling there.

"Starbuck?" Apollo said, anxiously watching his scanner.

"Yo." Starbuck's voice came through loud and clear over the comcircuit in Apollo's helmet.

"I don't know what it is," Apollo said, "but I'm getting the funny feeling that we're not alone out here."

Starbuck allowed his gaze to leave his instruments momentarily. He glanced over at Apollo's Viper flying alongside his. He had a gambler's instincts, and no gambler ever dismissed an intuitive feeling. Starbuck was well known for his gambler's luck, but there were times when Apollo's combat instincts overshadowed Starbuck's famous hunches, approaching clairvoyance.

"I've got nothing on my scanner," Starbuck said, tensing slightly.

Inside Apollo's cockpit, two warning blips appeared upon his scanner screen.

"Starbuck. . . ."

The other pilot knew that tone of voice only too well.

"Oh, oh . . ."

Starbuck licked his lips nervously, his gaze riveted to his scanner screen. It remained clear. He leaned forward slightly to adjust its directional mode, fine-tuning the range.

"I don't have a thing," he said. "There's nothing in front of us . . ."

"I'm on rear scan," Apollo said. "I've got two blips, behind us . . ."

"Swell. How close?" Starbuck switched to rear scan and it was at that precise moment that they came under fire as beams of energy, blindingly bright, lanced through space

7

all around them, narrowly missing both their ships. "That close, huh?"

"They're coming up on us fast," Apollo said. "And we don't have much fuel to spare for evasive action. It doesn't look too good. I'm going right..."

"I'll take left," said Starbuck, feeling the familiar surge of adrenaline kicking in. "Good luck, old buddy."

"We'll need it," Apollo said. "Dispatching automatic distress to fleet. Be seeing you..."

Apollo hit the switch that sent the distress call back to the *Galactica*. It would keep on transmitting until he shut it off or was blown to bits. A light on his console began to flash red as the call went out, even as both pilots, moving together like clockwork, rolled their Vipers in opposite directions, separating in an effort to avoid the laser fire of their pursuers.

Sheba swore to herself as she observed the two ships splitting up, rolling left and right. They were still too far away for her to get a clear visual on them, but she took no chances with Cylon fighters. The two ships she was pursuing with her wingmate, Bojay, would not slip away. She had fired as soon as they were in range and she was certain that she had not rushed her shot, yet she had missed. In spite of their advantage of surprise, the two ships had reacted almost instantaneously.

Almost as if they knew we were coming up on them, Sheba thought. It appeared that yahrens of fighting was beginning to make the Cylons better flyers. An unsettling thought. She heard Bojay's exclamation of surprise through her helmet's comcircuit and she knew that the sudden maneuver of their quarry had impressed him, as well. But there was no time to pay grudging respects to the enemy pilots for their flying ability. They both had their work cut out for them now that they had lost the advantage of surprise.

"I'll pick up the one on the right," Sheba said, angling her Viper to follow Apollo's craft.

Inside his cockpit, Bojay smiled and touched the horse-head insignia emblazoned on his helmet. It was a private thing with him, the gesture was his only superstition, but touching his helmet insignia was a way of hoping that the luck of his commander would be his own as well.

"The one on the left is as good as dead," said Bojay. "I'll be back to help you with the other one in half a flash."

"Assuming I'll need help," Sheba replied.

The pursuing Vipers separated, rolling to either side, and the chase was on. Coming in from behind gave Sheba and her wingmate an advantage. The one thing the Cylon fighters had in common with the design of the Vipers was that they had no firepower from the rear. Fighter craft were designed to be as light as possible, both for the sake of economy and because of all ships, the sleek fighter craft had the highest mortality rate. A lighter fighter craft was easier to prepare for battle and easier to launch with speed. Most of the ship's weight was in the fuel it carried. Fighters were designed for speed and maneuverability. Putting in aft laser batteries would have meant sacrificing precious weight and room for fuel. All a fighter was, was a vehicle for carrying a minimal amount of laser batteries as far and as quickly as possible within the limitations of its design. It carried no more and no less than was thought necessary to get the job done. Which, in their present circumstances, was fortunate for Bojay and Sheba, because that meant that so long as their quarry took evasive action, they could not fire. About the only way the enemy ships could return fire in their present predicament would be if they used their maneuvering jets to cause them to tumble, thereby reversing their positions, but that meant exposing a greater surface area while they were executing their tumbling maneuver, presenting a bigger target. Not even Cylons were that stupid.

The only chance they had was to continue their evasive action, in the hopes of causing Bojay and Sheba to fail to properly anticipate their flight paths. Then they might have a chance either to run for it or to attempt a reversal, getting in behind them. Sheba was not about to let that happen. Using every ounce of skill and intuition she had acquired from yahrens of combat experience, she matched the enemy ship move for move. And it took every ounce of skill, at that. Sheba bit her lower lip as she caught herself just in time to avoid getting faked out.

The bastard's good, she thought. Better than he's got any right to be. But most of the pressure was on him. He could not return her fire from his present position, and taking evasive action gave her a chance to close the distance between them, so long as she didn't make any mistakes.

Bojay was having just as rough a time of it. Just as he would get his opponent in his sights, the ship would dart to one side, causing his shot to go wide of the mark. He regretted his earlier boast that he would dispose of the ship in "half a flash." It was taking considerably longer than that. The pilot of the ship he chased was an absolutely first-rate flyer. Bojay shook his head. He hadn't seen anyone handle a fighter craft like that in yahrens. Not since...

As she closed with Apollo's ship, Sheba flipped a switch on her console that would enable her to pick up a lifeform reading on the enemy pilot. There was something bothering her. As the distance between the two ships lessened, she could see that there was something about that fighter's configuration that seemed very familiar, that seemed wrong.

Either the Cylons were suddenly using a brand new design or . . .

She stared at the scanner and her eyes grew wide as she saw the readout.

"LIFEFORMS . . . HUMAN . . . HUMAN . . . HUMAN . . ."

Bojay! She had to stop him before it was too late.

She shouted into her helmet mike. *"Bojay! Cease fire! Cease fire!"*

His voice came back to her over the comcircuit.

"Cease fire? Are you crazy? Cain'll have us for dinner if we let them get away! We've already reported contact and I'm right on—"

"They're human, Bojay!"

"What?"

"I said . . . they're *human!"*

Bojay wasn't sure he heard right.

"That's impossible," he said. "It's some sort of trick. A scanner malfunction . . ."

He flipped his own scanner to lifeform readout and was amazed at what he saw. It couldn't be. It just couldn't be.

"I don't believe it," he said softly.

Sheba's voice came back to him.

"Switching to unicom . . ."

She switched on the hailing frequency that would broadcast her message to the other ships. Vipers. They were Vipers!

"Attention," Sheba hailed the ships. "Attention . . . attention. . . . This is Silver Spar group leader commanding Viper pilots to slow to surrender. We are locked on target. . . ."

There was no mistaking the human voice that came over his comcircuit. Even as he contined evasive action, Starbuck's mind raced. Silver Spar Squadron? What the hell? It could easily be a trick, a vocal synthesizer, it had been tried before. Whoever they are, thought Starbuck, they're very good. Too good. No matter what he tried, he couldn't shake the pilot on his tail. He flipped his own rear scanner to lifeform readout. They *were* humans!

"Apollo!"

"I heard," Apollo said. "It checks, I've got them on scanner and they read human, but it could still be some sort of trick. The Cylons could have come up with something new we don't even know about. But there's no getting away, Starbuck. Whoever they are, they've got us."

He switched his comcircuit to unicom frequency.

"This is Captain Apollo, strike commander of the *Battlestar Galactica.* Who *are* you?"

He heard the woman's voice come back over his comcircuit, talking to her wingmate.

"Bojay?"

"I heard him. But it *can't* be. They're all dead. It can't possibly—"

Apollo heard Starbuck's voice cut in.

"Bojay?" Did she say *Bojay?*

"Starbuck!" The one called Bojay sounded as if he had just seen a ghost. "By all that's holy...."

Apollo heard the man called Bojay let out a whoop that almost deafened him.

"Apollo!" Starbuck's voice registered shock and disbelief. "It is, it's Bojay! Don't you remember? He was in our squadron until..."

Starbuck's voice trailed off.

"Until he transferred to the fifth fleet," Apollo finished for him. "I remember. And they were all wiped out in the Battle of Molecay."

"Two yahrens ago," said Starbuck. "But either they're not dead or . . ."

"We *are?*" said Apollo. "Don't go spacehappy on me, Starbuck. There's got to be some sort of rational explanation. Either way, they could've had us by now if they wanted us dead. I think we'd better do just as the lady said."

CHAPTER TWO

Flight Officer Tolen looked up from his screens on the command bridge of the *Pegasus*.

"Alert Commander Cain," he said to one of the officers standing by.

The patrol was escorting two ships back to the battlestar. Two Viper fighters! He switched the comcircuit to public address mode and sat stunned, along with the rest of the men and women on the bridge, as they listened to the exchange between the members of their patrol and the pilots of the two Vipers they were bringing in.

"Bojay"—the man whose voice came over the comcircuit was named Starbuck, a name that seemed to ring a bell with Tolen—"if that's really you, God, I can't believe it! Tell us what happened! How in hell did you survive?"

Sheba's voice cut in.

"You will maintain silence until we've landed aboard the *Battlestar Pegasus*."

"The *Pegasus!*" The new voice Tolen heard was Apollo's. They were disregarding Sheba's order to maintain silence. Under the circumstances, Tolen thought, he could hardly blame them. It had to have been as much of a shock to them as it was to him. "That's just not possible," said Apollo.

"The *Pegasus* was Cain's ship," said Starbuck.

"The greatest military commander of them all," replied Apollo. "He was my idol."

Sheba's irate voice cut in once more.

"Your idol will order you blasted to space debris if you don't shut off your transmitter. In case you clowns don't know it, we're in a sector controlled by the Cylons."

"Oh, my Lord. . . ." Apollo went on as if he hadn't heard her. They had just come within visual range of the *Pegasus,* floating majestically in space. "It isn't a dream," Apollo said in an awestruck voice, "it *is* the *Pegasus!* Commander Cain's flagship!"

The *Battlestar Pegasus* was a sister ship to the *Galactica* and looked identical to Adama's ship in every way, except for the fact that the *Pegasus* was slightly older, having been commissioned several yahrens before Adama's battlestar. As they approached the *Pegasus,* Apollo and Starbuck could see the difference between her and their own base ship. The *Pegasus* was scarred. They could see where she had taken some severe damage amidships, damage that had been repaired, but still it was the sort of damage that would have sent any other battlestar back for refitting. Only there was no longer anywhere to go for that. Her hull was creased and pitted, burned in many places. The *Pegasus* looked like an old, embattled warrior. Ships of the battlestar class were the finest achievements of the colony worlds, marvels of sophisticated technology that were capable of taking an incredible amount of abuse, and from what they could see of the *Pegasus*, it was clear to both Starbuck and Apollo that Cain had been none too gentle with her.

"By the Lords of Kobol," Starbuck said, "will you look at that! What in God's name is holding her together—spit?"

Inside her Viper, Sheba clenched her fists, furious with the Viper pilots they were shepherding back to the *Pegasus*. They were acting like two awestruck rookies.

"They won't shut up," she said. Tolen wasn't sure if she was addressing her remarks to him or to Bojay. "They're acting as if they've just seen an apparition."

"I'm still not sure I haven't," said Apollo.

Tolen knew that Cain was doubtless listening in his quarters. He wondered what the commander made of this development. Here they were, fighting for their lives in the middle of Cylon controlled territory, and two strange Vipers appear out of nowhere. Where had they come from? The voices of the two pilots seemed human, but Cylons were very devious opponents. It could be some sort of ruse, a trick to sneak two mock Viper fighters aboard the *Pegasus*. There could even be some sort of explosive devices. . . . Just to be safe, Tolen ordered a full complement of warriors to the landing bay.

The four fighters slowed, using their forward thrusters to brake as they made their landing approach. They lined up on the hatchway and waited for the go-ahead from the bridge of the battlestar. Cautiously, Tolen gave them their clearance.

One at a time, they eased their ships forward toward the giant hatchway with the glowing perimeter, the landing bay with its force field that kept the warm molecules of air inside from escaping into space. As each Viper approached the force field, millimicrons before contact, the black boxes wired into their onboard computers were triggered off automatically. The force field's perimeter indicator lights strobed briefly, rapidly, as the ships passed through the force field, as if through a semi-permeable membrane. The entrance of the craft was accompanied by a popping sound as a little of the atmosphere inside escaped, although not enough to affect the environment inside the landing bay. The ground crews inside the landing bay directed them where to land their Vipers and in a short time the pilots were raising their cockpit domes and stepping out into the mob of warriors who surrounded them.

Apollo alighted on the deck, shaking his head with disbelief.

"It's like some sort of miracle, seeing all you guys," he said.

Bojay came up to him and held out his hand. They shook, each staring at the other with a mixture of astonishment and bewilderment.

"Imagine how *we* feel," said Bojay. "More than two yahrens ago, we set off to attempt to save Molecay and its satellites from the Cylons. Since then, we haven't seen a single human soul."

"Then the rest of the fifth fleet was . . . ?"

"Destroyed," said Bojay grimly. "We're all that's left. Thanks to Cain. If it wasn't for the old man, we'd be gone too."

Starbuck had worked his way through the press of bodies to join them. He and Bojay both let out shouts of delight and hugged each other, clapping each other on the back as if the physical contact would assure each man that the other was real.

"You had to have headed away from the colonies to be this far out," said Starbuck. "Why?"

"Cain's idea," Bojay said. "He knew the Cylons would be lined up from Molecay to the colonies, just waiting for us. So he took a heading toward deep space and kept right on going. There was nowhere else *to* go. We haven't stopped fighting since."

"Running, you mean," said Apollo, appreciating their plight only too well.

"Run?" Bojay turned to face him with an ironic smile. "Cain? He doesn't know the meaning of the word. We're flying strike missions around the clock."

"Strike missions?" Starbuck stared at him. "For two yahrens, you've been on full strike status? *With what?* What do you use for supplies?"

It had been all the *Galactica* could do just to keep on running. She had to stop wherever possible, anywhere where they could beg supplies or scavenge raw materials. Even so, it had been necessary to cannibalize many of the smaller ships in order to enable them to keep on going. And it was all they could do to manage to defend themselves. Yet, the *Pegasus* was all alone. And on full strike status. *On the offensive!*

"You might say we requisition our supplies from the Cylons, Mr. Starbuck," said a new voice.

Tolen had been standing at the edge of the crowd, listening to the conversation. He had gone unnoticed, but at the sound of his voice, the men and women of the *Pegasus* cleared a way for him. He approached the two pilots from the *Galactica*.

"Gentlemen," he nodded a greeting. "Flight Officer Tolen. I'm sure you have a lot of questions, but right now Commander Cain would like to see you both in his quarters.

If you would follow me, please?"

Starbuck and Apollo exchanged glances, then moved off to follow Tolen. Starbuck spoke softly to Apollo as they crossed the wide expanse of the landing bay.

"I grew up on stories of Commander Cain," he said. "The Juggernaut, they called him."

Apollo nodded. Cain had already been a celebrated hero when he was just a boy, dreaming of becoming a warrior someday.

"It'll be like meeting a legend," he said.

On the way to Cain's private quarters, both men kept glancing all around them, taking in the condition of the battlestar, observing the members of her crew.

News of their arrival had obviously spread like wildfire throughout the ship. They were stared at by everyone they passed. Many of the crew members looked as though they would have liked to engage them in conversation, but the presence of Tolen made it clear where he was taking them. It was clear that no one kept Commander Cain waiting.

There was no need for the two of them to speak. Besides having been rendered speechless, each man knew what the other was thinking.

For two yahrens, the *Pegasus* had been waging war against the Cylons all by herself. Yet, in spite of that, in spite of the battle-worn external appearance she presented, the battlestar was maintained in a condition to stand a fleet inspection. There was no war-weariness on the faces of the crew they passed. There was a crispness to their movements, a spit-and-polish aspect to their demeanor. The crew of the *Pegasus*, allowing for the inevitable deprivation caused by the lack of fleet supply, appeared ready to turn out on parade. Cain obviously ran a tight ship and military discipline was rigidly maintained. It became increasingly clear to Starbuck and Apollo how the crew of the *Pegasus* were able to withstand such a long and impossibly demanding struggle. They drew on the iron will of their commander.

After all, Apollo thought, they were all serving under the command of a living legend. They had a lot to live up to.

By the time they reached Cain's quarters, Apollo discovered that his palms were sweating. He was about to meet his childhood hero. He felt, suddenly, very young and very green. Tolen buzzèd to announce their arrival. From within, Cain bid them enter.

The accommodations were not what they would have expected for the commander of a battlestar. It was true that aboard the *Galactica,* Adama's quarters were far from luxurious, but Cain's cabin was positively spartan. Except for the fact that it was larger and had a console with multiple screens, a sitting alcove, a large and comfortable chair that was obviously the sole privilege of rank that Cain allowed himself, and a window to space, the cabin was no different from that of any warrior's. The window, not shielded for the moment, afforded a wide view of the stars, and the lights inside the cabin were very dim. A man stood with his back to them, silhouetted against the panoramic window. He was dressed in a uniform identical to theirs, that of a Viper pilot. He turned around and faced them, but he was still in shadow and they couldn't clearly see his features.

"Get our visitors something to drink, Tolen," he said. "They look a little pale."

With a slight movement of his head, he indicated the sitting alcove.

"Make yourselves comfortable, gentlemen," he said. "I believe in discipline, but I don't stand on ceremony. Besides, you don't look all that steady on your feet."

The two men took their seats. Apollo licked his lips nervously.

"It's an honor to meet you, Commander," he said. "A very great honor."

"Yes, I should imagine that it is," came the reply.

Apollo had no idea what to say to that. There was a moment of awkward silence.

"A slight attempt at humor, Captain," Cain said. "You'll have to excuse me, but I never did get used to having people stare at me and treat me as if I were some sort of god. I'm not. I'm just a soldier. A warrior, like yourself. As it happens, I'm a good one, but I'm still only flesh and blood."

It was, if anything, an understatement of incredible proportions. As Cain stepped forward into the light, they could see that his simple uniform bore more decorations than either of them had ever seen, including the Gold Cluster he wore at his throat over an ascot scarf, his sole affectation. The Cluster was not bestowed on anyone who was merely a good soldier. To wear the gold, it took heroism.

It felt somehow unreal to Apollo, to finally meet his idol face-to-face, a man he had considered long dead. Cain was not a tall man. He was of average height, muscular, with iron-gray hair. His strikingly blue eyes were his most prominent feature. Their gaze was uncomfortably direct. His face seemed to have been carved from granite. He was a handsome man, no longer young, but still ramrod straight and every inch a leader.

"I had thought that I would never see another human face," said Cain, "with the exception of my people on the *Pegasus*. Yet, there you are. The question is, where in Kobol did you come from?"

"From the *Galactica*, sir," said Apollo. He felt uncomfortable sitting in Cain's presence. "Under the command of—"

"Adama?"

Cain moved forward suddenly, staring intently at Apollo.

"Yes, sir. My father."

"Yes. . . . Yes, I can see the resemblance now. So you're Adama's boy. How is the old modocker?"

"Well," said Apollo, "considering the load he's carried since the destruction of our nation."

Cain nodded. "Yes, I can well imagine. And the rest of the fleet?"

"Only the *Galactica* survived, sir. Along with some hundred and twenty-odd ships of various classifications carrying what's left of our people."

"My God," said Cain. "I thought *we* had it bad. Only one hundred and twenty ships? That's *all* that's left from all the colonies?"

Apollo nodded.

Cain seemed lost in thought for several moments.

"There was a certain young lady . . ." he said, almost to himself.

He moved toward his desk, upon which stood a small hologram projector. There was an intense quality to his voice as he spoke, as if he wanted to know the truth, but was at the same time afraid to know.

"Out of all those people from the colonies," he said softly, "I suppose it's quite unlikely that she would be among the few survivors. Still . . ."

His hand reached out toward the projector, then hovered above it uncertainly.

"What was her name?" Starbuck asked gently.

"Her name was Cassiopea," Cain said.

As he spoke, he turned on the projector and a column of diffused light appeared in the center of the cabin. Cain punched in the projection and a holographic image of Cassiopea appeared. Apollo heard the sharp intake of Starbuck's breath. The image of Cassiopea cocked her head and smiled.

"I'll never forget you, you old wardaggit," she said. "Hurry back. Hurry back to me."

The image disappeared.

The two men sat stunned into silence. There was no mistaking the look on Cassiopea's face, no mistaking the inflection in her voice. Yet, she had never mentioned knowing Cain to them. And then again, neither of them had ever asked.

Starbuck thought back to the first time they had met. It had been shortly after Caprica had been destroyed. Even as the Cylons sued for peace, their base ships had moved into position to attack the colonies. By the time their treachery had been discovered, it had been too late.

Among the handful of survivors Adama had gathered together, there had been a woman who had been a socialator, a highly skilled courtesan and paid companion. There was as much separating a socialator from a common prostitute as there was separating a Viper from a shuttlecraft, a seasoned warrior from a green cadet. It was an old and honored profession, but there were still those who did not appreciate the difference between women of Cassiopea's profession and whores. Starbuck had told himself at the time that he had removed Cassiopea from their presence because she had a broken arm and required medical attention, and because the people she had fallen in with had not desired her company and had been abusing her. But there had been more to it than that. Much more.

He had no claim on Cassiopea, but the thought of competition in the form of Commander Cain disturbed him greatly. What was it Apollo had called him—a living legend? How do you compete with that?

"I can see she's had the same effect on you gentlemen

that she's always had on me," said Cain, misinterpreting their silence. "Apparently you've never seen her before."

He looked away from them, back at the projector. It seemed to the two pilots that Cain felt embarrassed at having revealed his feelings to them. Before either of them had a chance to speak, Cain quickly changed the subject.

"Speaking of lovely ladies," he said, "have you met my daughter?"

Cain punched in another projection and a holographic image of a young, long-legged brunette with flashing dark eyes appeared. She was as lovely as Cassiopea in her own way. She had a dark, smoldering beauty, an aggressive bearing.

"Happy birthday, Father," she said. "I love you. I'm the luckiest daughter in the cosmos."

If there was more to the message, they didn't hear it because Cain shut off the projector at that point.

"If I'd met that young lady," said Apollo, "I would most certainly have remembered."

"Her voice sounds a bit familiar, though," said Starbuck.

Cain chuckled.

"It should. She's the pilot who almost flew you right out of your britches, Captain Apollo. Like father, like daughter, wouldn't you say? She's the best damn Viper pilot on the *Pegasus.*"

"You'll hear no argument from me," said Apollo, recalling all too well the sinking feeling he had experienced when he had realized that nothing he could do would shake the fighter that pursued him. Had she been a Cylon, he would have been blown to space dust.

Cain smiled again and turned back toward the window, as if seeking something out there.

"Adama," he said softly. "Who would have guessed it?

The *Galactica* is sure going to be a sight for these sore eyes. The two of us together once again, on the offensive. Full strike against the Cylons!"

He turned back to face Starbuck and Apollo.

"Gentlemen," he said, "I believe our troubles are over. The Empire is about to fall."

CHAPTER THREE

Adama was bone weary. Had his hair not turned prematurely white many years ago, it would most certainly have been that shade by now, a result of the rigors of command. And it was more than just the pressure of command that was making Adama feel his age as he never had before. Although he was not a young man anymore, Adama was able to draw on reserves of energy that not even the youngest warriors under his command could match. He had to. The burden of command he carried as chief officer of a battlestar was nothing compared to the weight of the responsibility he bore. The task of shepherding a rag-tag fleet of ships that had never been designed for duty in deep space on a journey of incalculable length was severe enough without having to worry about the constant pursuit of the Cylon Empire.

They were relentless. Their leaders had vowed to exterminate the human race, and the Cylon warriors were tireless in their efforts to carry out the commands of their superiors. Indeed, they could not tire. They were like drone missiles, programmed to destroy and they would carry out their programming or die fighting. It was all they knew. Such a singleminded purpose made them the most formidable foes that humans ever had to face.

Perhaps, had they been anything but Cylons, Adama might have felt an admiration for their ceaseless efforts; he might have felt the respect of a soldier for a worthy enemy. But Adama could summon up no feelings of respect for a machine society where the concept of free will was completely alien. Alien. It was an apt term to describe the Cylons. They were the most alien creatures Adama had ever come across. Humans could not even begin to understand them. What little they knew of the Cylon race was frightening enough. What they did not know was terrifying in its implications.

The structure of Cylon society seemed to have much in common with that of insects. The lowliest level of Cylon society, at least that which humans had come across, were their warriors. A Cylon warrior was little more than a machine. Indeed, they even resembled robots in their armor and no one was really certain where the armor ended and the being began. Cylons were like cybernetic organisms. Living beings made part machine by the armor that they wore. Each and every Cylon, by virtue of its sophisticated armor, was part of a vast communications network. They were like pawns, moved about on some massive chessboard by their leaders. Yet the very size of their organization was a handicap to them. With so much information coming in, their leaders could react only to the extent that they could sort the input and assign priorities. Even though the Cylon leaders were said to have several brains to assist them in this task, it was fortunate for Adama that they were not computers. They could make mistakes.

Cylons were slow to take action on their own. Their dependence on their leaders gave humans an advantage. Cylons had nothing resembling human initiative. In battle, they were ruthlessly methodical, but human pilots were capable of improvising, of using their intuition. In a one-on-one encounter, a Cylon fighter was no match for a Viper, but Cylons did not fight one-on-one. In battle, their warriors were like a series circuit, each one functioning with all the others like a unit. It was this which made their pinwheel attacks so devastating. It took pilots like Starbuck and Apollo yahrens to learn each other's reactions and response times well enough to enable them to work together like a single unit. Cylons did it automatically.

Adama could almost understand why they considered humans such a threat. Their idea of perfection stemmed from a society in which individuality was sacrificed to the ideal of the common good. There had been, in ages past, human philosophers who had expressed similar ideals, but the Cylons had taken such principles to their furthest extreme. In Cylon society, the individual did not exist. Each separate organism was but a cog in the massive Cylon machine. As such, they had certainly achieved order, but at a price no human would ever be willing to pay. And it was for that reason, Adama felt certain, that the Cylon leaders ordered all humans to be exterminated. It was not enough for them to destroy the colony worlds. Humanity had to be wiped out completely, totally. Not one could survive.

Adama often wondered why, if the Cylons had achieved perfection as they claimed, they feared humans so. He thought he knew the answer, but he could take no comfort in it.

Adama's task had come down to a single dictum. Survive. At any cost, survive. He could not allow himself to lose hope. He had to be strong, so that the others would have confidence and would not lose hope. Yet, in their present predicament, it was very hard to remain optimistic. They were faced with seemingly insurmountable odds. Added to that, the latest status reports were far from encouraging.

"We're down to the last of it, Skipper," said Flight Sergeant Jolly. "I've checked every ship in the fleet. Everyone's down to life support now. Unless we come to a dead stop..."

Adama wanted to close his eyes and just not deal with it anymore. It took all his effort to remain composed as he stood before his monitor screens on the *Galactica*'s command bridge. Once again they were faced with disaster, but Adama could not allow his fears to show. He was the commander. His people would be looking to him to find a solution. The only thing Adama could look to was his faith.

"Thank you, Sergeant Jolly," he said, shutting off the monitor. There was nothing more to say.

Colonel Tigh came up beside him. Adama turned to him, thankful for his presence. There was only so much frustration he could keep bottled up inside.

"Well, that's just fine," he said. "To have come all this way to simply run out of fuel...."

"That isn't the worst of it," said Tigh, wishing that he could have brought his commander some encouraging news, but the news he did have was all bad.

"Oh?" said Adama. "You mean leaving ships behind, cannibalizing them to what extent we could and doubling people to what miserable quarters we have isn't the worst of it? What could possibly be worse?"

"We're picking up unusual communication traffic, sir," said Tigh.

Adama frowned. "But that means we could be close to a civilization."

"Yes, sir. But the transmissions are Cylon."

"Good Lord," said Adama. "Just what we need. We're down to our last supplies of fuel and we're picking up transmissions from a base star."

"No, sir, not a base star," Tigh replied. "Much of what we're hearing is civilian."

"Civilian? But we're a full star system away from Cylon!"

"I know, Commander. I can't explain it, but there's no arguing with what we're picking up." Tigh took a deep breath. "Somewhere out there, not too far away, is a city. A Cylon city."

Omega approached just as Tigh was completing his statement.

"That could explain why our scouting patrol is so long overdue," Omega said.

"Who was flying the mission?" asked Adama, fearing the worst.

"Starbuck and Apollo, sir," said Tigh.

Adama turned away from them, not wishing them to see the expression on his face.

"How long before the patrol would have exhausted their fuel?" he said.

"If they've been flying continuously since launch," said Tigh, "they'd be out of fuel by now."

Adama sagged against the console. He clenched his fist and raised it slightly, then let his hand fall against his side.

"Then it's over," he said softly.

Tigh and Omega exchanged glances. They could understand what Adama was feeling at that moment. They had both lost family in the war with the Cylons.

"Sir," said Tigh, "perhaps if we launched a shuttle probe—"

Adama straightened and turned to face them. He realized that there was nothing he could do for Starbuck and Apollo. He had the fleet to think of now.

"We have no fuel to spare to be searching for two warriors. We have to conserve every bit of fuel we have to maintain life support systems in the fleet. List the scouting patrol as missing in action."

Flight Officer Rigel looked up from the scanner screens.

"Sir? I'm picking up something very odd. . . ."

"What is it?" said Tigh, moving to the scanner screens.

"I don't know. It seems to be some sort of echo effect, perhaps the *Galactica*'s image bouncing off some ion field. . . ."

Tigh shook his head.

"I'll handle it, Commander," he said. "She's new on scan, I'll take a look at whatever it is she's picking up. Feed it to the bridge monitors, Rigel."

An image of the scanner readout appeared on the large bridge monitor screens. Adama and Tigh both stared at it. Rigel had been right. The image did, indeed, resemble a battlestar. Tigh leaned forward and contacted the maintenance crew over the ship's intercom.

"Have this scanner turret checked immediately," he said. "We obviously have some sort of malfunction, Commander. Control . . . shift to high resolution. . . ."

After a momentary hesitation, the image on the monitor screens seemed to jump, growing larger and more clear. There was no doubt about it. It was a battlestar. But that was clearly impossible.

"If that's an echo," said Adama, "it's the cleanest transmission I've ever seen."

Tigh shook his head. "We must be picking up some old transmission, Commander. Something that's been bouncing around for yahrens, it's the only explanation that makes sense. Nevertheless..."

Omega, face pale, looked up from the console.

"Sir, signal coming in on fleet comline Alpha!"

Adama turned a frankly disbelieving gaze on Omega.

"That's impossible. The Alpha line is an automatic scramble communicator between warships, and we're the only surviving warship left. Check your systems, there must be—"

At that moment, the image on the monitor screens was replaced by the face of Commander Cain.

"Well, Adama, you old wardaggit, I might have known I'd find you and your fleet sitting dead on its ass."

Adama stared at the screen, eyes wide with shock. Slowly, he sank into his command chair.

"Cain! By all that's holy..."

Cain chuckled. "Nothing holy about me, old friend. What's the matter? You look as though you've seen a ghost. I can't be looking that bad."

The crew of the bridge all gathered around Adama, staring at the monitor screens. There wasn't one of them who hadn't heard of Commander Cain. Yet, according to all reports, his ship had perished over two yahrens ago.

The screens showed Cain sitting casually in his command chair on the bridge of the *Pegasus,* his leg draped over the arm of his chair. With one hand, he was holding a swagger stick and absently tapping it against his boot.

"Adama! Wake up, man. Are you just going to sit there and let me plow through your whole fleet or do I get some sort of rendezvous instructions?"

Adama finally overcame the shock of seeing a man he had thought long dead.

"Yes, yes, of course. Colonel Tigh, make ready to board Commander Cain and position the *Pegasus* to defend our flank. It's a miracle, Cain. A blessed miracle..."

"I make my own miracles," Cain replied dryly. "But have it your way. I'll be aboard in a few centons."

"And I'll have some vintage Ambrosa waiting for you," Adama said.

Cain grinned. "Well, I should think so."

His image disappeared from the screens.

Tigh shook his head. "My God. He's alive. I thought he perished with the fifth fleet more than two yahrens ago."

"That's the fabric of miracles, Colonel," said Adama, "the impossible. Once again, we're delivered."

The men and women on the bridge broke into cheers and wild applause.

The doors of the shuttle opened and Cain stepped out onto the landing deck of the *Galactica*, accompanied by two warriors in full dress. The throng that packed the landing bay cheered his arrival. They were like a family greeting a long lost prodigal son. Adama rushed up to Cain and embraced him.

"God bless you, old friend," he said. "You don't know how I feel at this moment. I'm at a loss for words."

"Me too," said Cain. He clapped Adama on the shoulder. "It's good to see you once again, old friend. And I have a present for you to mark the occasion." He turned to one of his aides. "Where are those space loiterers we picked up? Front and center!"

Adama could not believe his eyes when he saw his son and Starbuck emerging from the shuttle. He fought back tears as he embraced Apollo.

"Son! I thought I'd seen the last of you."

"You would have, too," said Cain, "if my daughter hadn't cut them off when she did. They were headed right for Gomoray."

"Gomoray? I had no idea we were so close to the Delphian Empire!"

"It *was* the Delphian Empire," said Cain. "It is now the newest colony of the Cylon Empire. They've turned it into a model of machine efficiency."

"But . . . that was a society of some fifty million living beings," said Adama.

Cain shook his head. "Not anymore."

There was stunned silence on the landing deck as the import of his words sank in. The Cylons had exterminated an entire species.

"Guess you're a little out of touch with life on the front lines," said Cain. "Well. . . . Come on, old friend, where's that Ambrosa you promised me?"

In Commander Adama's private quarters, a subdued Commander Cain sat opposite his friend, his fingers toying with the stem of his drinking glass.

"When the fifth fleet was destroyed," said Cain, "I took every survivor I could aboard the *Pegasus* and headed straight for Gomoray, their most recent supply base. There was nowhere else to go. Any attempt to get back to the colonies would have resulted in the destruction of my ship.

It was what the Cylons expected me to try. So I set course for Gomoray, only when we arrived, it was to discover that the Delphians had been wiped out by the Cylons. Fortunately, it's only a recently established colony of theirs and nowhere near being at full strength. We've managed to survive by living off them ever since, like pirates. There was nothing else to do. We needed to hit them for supplies and I simply couldn't risk going back."

"It's incredible," said Adama. "If they've conquered Gomoray, then that means they wield power halfway across the universe."

Cain nodded. "We're surrounded. The only thing I've been able to do is keep hitting their base as often as I can so they can't build up enough to launch a full strike against me. I've been very lucky. What I've never understood is why they haven't sent for a force of base ships to finish us off. Now it's quite clear why they didn't."

"You mean we're the reason."

"It all makes sense now," Cain said. "I could never understand it before, but now I see that this rebel fleet of yours must have received first priority. They obviously want you very badly. I was never able to break their code. I had no idea there were other survivors."

"Nor did I," Adama said. "Your arrival has been a tremendous lift for all our people."

"And a deathblow to the Cylons," Cain said grimly. "We can take them now, Adama! This is the turning point!"

Adama shook his head.

"My old friend. . . . All we can hope to take from the Cylons is much needed fuel. A military victory is out of the question."

Cain frowned. "What are you talking about? I've had them on their knees in this sector with just *one* battlestar!

With two, I can *finish* them! At least on Gomoray."

"And then what?"

"Then we'll have all the fuel we need," said Cain, setting his glass down so hard that it broke. "And a base from which to strike!"

Adama sighed. Cain hadn't changed. As always, he was too eager, too ready to throw all cautions to the winds.

"Cain, we cannot secure this planet. Those base ships that haven't bothered you are after me *en masse*. Our only hope is to raid them for fuel and then move on."

Cain stared at Adama for a long time.

"You mean, run?" he said at last.

"I mean escape."

"But why, dammit? We can outfly them. We can outfight them. We can—"

"In case you haven't noticed," Adama interrupted him, "I'm protecting a hundred and twenty ships that are only capable of crawling along at speeds that aren't good for anything but target practice. Maybe you can outfly them, Cain. But I can't."

"There has to be another way," said Cain.

"There isn't. But your knowledge of the Cylon supply lines will be invaluable. If we could intercept several of their tankers—"

"Why bother with tankers?" said Cain. "Why not hit the fuel base on Gomoray?"

"I'm low on fuel," Adama said. "We're barely able to sustain life support systems as it is. I can't leave these ships without protection while I take on an entire planet with nothing but my fuel reserves."

"So don't," Cain said. "Just give me a couple of your best squadrons and I'll take that fuel depot myself."

"I'll be happy to settle for enough to get us out of here,"

Adama said. "You prepare the battle plan to hit their tankers, I'll approve it. Meanwhile, enjoy a few centons of hospitality aboard the *Galactica*. Kobol knows, you deserve it."

Cain nodded, although he clearly wasn't pleased.

"Very well, Adama. If that's the way you want it."

"That's the way it has to be," Adama said. "I have no choice."

CHAPTER FOUR

Apollo and Starbuck walked rapidly down a corridor in the *Galactica*'s living quarters, heading for Cassiopea's cabin.

"What are you going to do?" Apollo asked his friend.

"Find some way to let him down easy," said Starbuck. "You don't just dump on a national hero."

"You're assuming Cassiopea isn't going to be as excited as everyone else in the fleet that he's back. Perhaps she knows already—it's all over the ship."

They stopped at her door.

"Apollo," Starbuck said.

"Oh, yes, that's right," said Apollo, looking at his friend with a perfectly straight face. "I forgot. Once they've experienced Starbuck's famous charm..."

"Come on, stow it, will you? That wasn't what I meant and you know it. But let's face it, he is an older man. And whatever it was they had between them was a long time ago."

Starbuck buzzed to announce his arrival.

"You're on your own," said Apollo. "Good luck."

Starbuck entered.

Cassiopea was not alone. She was spending some time with Boxey and his mechanized daggit. It was hard for children aboard the *Galactica*. There were not many of them in the rag-tag fleet, and all the adults were very aware of the fact that it was crucial in their development for them to have some time in which to *be* children. So they all made time for the little ones whenever they could. Their chances for survival were not great, but still, they were humanity's hope for the future.

"Starbuck!"

She jumped up and hugged him, giving him a friendly kiss. Starbuck had a feeling that it would have been considerably more friendly were it not for Boxey's presence.

"Hi, Starbuck!" Boxey jumped up and ran to his side. "Is my father back?"

Suddenly, Starbuck did not feel quite so self-confident as he did moments ago."

"Yeah, kid. He is."

Something in his tone alerted the sensitive Boxey to the fact that something was amiss.

"What's the matter?" cried the boy, suddenly anxious. "He's not hurt, is he?"

"No, no, nothing like that," said Starbuck.

"Come on, Muffey," Boxey said to his daggit droid. "We're going to find Dad."

He charged out of the room, his robot pet skittering after him as fast as it was able.

"Starbuck," Cassiopea said, when they were alone. "What is it? I can tell something's bothering you. What's wrong?"

Starbuck forgot the carefully rehearsed speech he had been going to make. What he said came out disjointed, awkward.

"I have some news for you," he said. "It's about an old friend of yours. Someone you may have been involved with. Or maybe someone you just liked, I don't know, but at any rate, he's been found alive—"

"Starbuck, what are you talking about?" she said. "Who's been found alive?"

"Look, I know it's all over between you, but we have to find some way to let him down easy. If you want to do it, fine. But I'll be glad to handle it for you if you think it's going to be too awkward...."

"Starbuck, will you get to the point? Who are we talking about?"

"Commander Cain."

Starbuck had never counted on her reaction. It seemed as if all the breath had been knocked out of her and, for the briefest moment, her eyes seemed to glaze. Then she bolted past him and ran out into the hall, moving quickly down the corridor. Starbuck could only stare after her stupidly.

Apollo was on the bridge, having a reunion with his son when Starbuck entered.

"Well? How'd she take the news?" Apollo said.

"Worse than I thought. She wanted to be alone."

Apollo fixed Starbuck with a steady gaze. He knew his friend too well not to be able to tell when Starbuck wasn't being entirely honest with him.

"Hey," he said, "it's me, Apollo, remember? I'm your friend. Friends are supposed to be able to talk."

Starbuck nodded. "Yeah, well. . . . I guess I just don't like to admit to anyone that I'm capable of forming attachments."

"You don't even like to admit it to yourself," Apollo said. "I've never understood that about you."

Starbuck sat down in one of the chairs behind the console.

"You were always part of a big family," he said. "I never had that. I just grew up keeping the number of people around me as large as I could."

"So that you couldn't get hurt by any particular one," said Apollo. "Starbuck, there's nothing wrong with feeling vulnerable."

"It isn't that I care if Cassiopea feels something for Cain," he said, trying to shrug it off, "it's just that I can't see it. He's . . . he's . . ."

"Too old? Better read up on your Book of the Word," said Apollo. "Some of the Elders of Kobol were sealed to some very young wives."

"Wives? Aren't we getting a little ahead of ourselves? She couldn't . . . she wouldn't *marry* him! Anyway, who cares? Certainly not me."

Starbuck got up and left the bridge, walking quickly.

"Poor Starbuck," said Boxey, who had heard every word and understood an awful lot for one so young. "Oh, well. He still has Athena. And Miran. And Noday and—"

"That'll be enough of that," Apollo said. "Who told you to listen, anyway?"

Cain was relaxing in his guest quarters aboard the *Galactica,* a cabin that had been vacated temporarily for him.

What with the way things had been, there was no surplus of accommodations aboard the battlestar. He was finishing off the bottle of Ambrosa Adama had given him as a gift when the buzzer announced a caller.

"Enter."

He got up and adjusted his scarf. Then froze. Cassiopea stood in the doorway.

"Cassi..." he said in a voice that was little more than a whisper.

There were tears in her eyes. Hesitantly, they moved toward one another, then they were in each other's arms, her head buried against his chest. Cain hugged her close, brushing his mouth against her hair.

"I thought you were dead," he said. "I'd given up hope...."

"Oh, I've missed you," Cassiopea said. "I had to force myself to stop thinking about you. I—"

Abruptly, she pulled away.

"I understand," Cain said quietly. "I couldn't have expected you to wait. It wouldn't have been fair. Especially with all those young warriors around. They're all madly in love with you, I'm sure."

"No, only one," she said. "And he does not love easily."

"Then don't waste your time on him."

She shook her head. "He's not a waste of time. He's just afraid of caring too much. Sometimes he reminds me of you. He had a pretty rough childhood."

"No worse than yours, I'm sure," said Cain.

She sighed. "We all handle loneliness in our own ways. My way was to reach out to everyone. Starbuck's was to shut everybody out."

"Starbuck." Cain thought back to the time aboard the *Pegasus*, when he had shown them a holographic image of

Cassiopea. He had thought they didn't know her. But now he could see why they hadn't said anything. He wondered what Starbuck must have felt at the time.

"He's a great warrior," Cassiopea said. "One of the finest pilots we have. Perhaps the best."

"He is, huh?" Cain smiled. It was clear she was no longer his. But then, he would have been a fool to have expected anything else. He was just overjoyed to see she was alive.

"I wasn't comparing the two of you," she said defensively. "You're going to have to give me some time to think. It's all just too much right now."

"We may not have much time," said Cain.

She nodded. "I know. What about Sheba? Is she . . . ?"

"She's grown up to be a beautiful young woman," Cain said. "And the finest fighter pilot in the fleet."

"I have a feeling she won't be very happy to hear that I've returned from the dead," Cassiopea said.

"No, perhaps not. Children don't understand the needs a man can have at different times of his life. You came into mine just after her mother died. It may have been difficult for her, but if it weren't for you. . . ."

"You don't have to say it," Cassiopea said. "But did you ever stop to think that maybe Sheba wanted to fill that role?"

"She's my daughter."

Cassiopea smiled. "I could be your daughter, as well."

"You could be. But you aren't."

"It isn't as cut and dried as you make it out to be," said Cassiopea. "If all you were looking for was physical fulfillment, companionship to keep you from feeling lonely, any socialator would have done as well."

"You know there was more to it than that, Cassi."

"Yes, I know. And so did Sheba. Because of that, I was a threat to her."

"She's a grown woman now, Cassi. I'm sure she understands."

"I wish I could be so sure. We're almost the same age. Because I was able to give you something Sheba never could, besides physical love, she resented me. Is there any reason for her to feel differently now?"

Cain looked into her eyes. "I don't know, Cassi. I guess a lot of that depends on you."

The Officers' Club aboard the *Galactica* was crowded as the pilots from both ships gathered together to celebrate their reunion. The center of attraction was a tall, vibrantly beautiful young woman who piloted one of the Vipers from the *Pegasus*.

"Our basic strategy," said Sheba, "has been to keep attacking the Cylon base on Gomoray. Hitting them as often as we can, as hard as we can, giving them as little opportunity to regroup as possible. Every time they manage to rebuild, we go in and turn their ground base to scrap metal. It's the only way we've been able to survive, to keep them constantly on the defensive."

"I want to hear from the pilots of the *Galactica*," said Bojay. "You must be keeping the tinheads pretty busy yourselves."

Apollo moved up to their table and took a chair.

"Sure," he said. "Just last week, we shot down a Cylon patrol ship. Mind if I join you?"

Sheba looked him over.

"My name is Apollo. Strike Captain Apollo. I believe you spent a lot of time on my tail. You *are* Sheba, aren't you?"

She smiled. "Yes. To both questions."

"Surely you weren't serious about shooting down just

one Cylon patrol ship in a whole week," said Bojay.

"Very serious," replied Apollo. "When you're responsible for the lives of hundreds of civilians crammed aboard slow-moving barges, you have to learn to keep a low profile."

"It sounds like we're going to be incompatible," said Sheba dryly.

"We all have to learn to adjust," Apollo said patiently. "Even the legendary Commander Cain may have to alter his combat techniques."

Sheba snorted. "And who's going to tell him that?"

"Being something of a student of your father's battle tactics," said Apollo, "I think he'll arrive at that decision on his own. If not, well..."

Tolen entered the Officers' Club at that moment and called the pilots to attention. They all jumped to their feet as Cain entered with his guard. He was accompanied by Cassiopea.

"No, no," protested Cain. "Please, resume your seats. We're not on duty now. This is supposed to be a party."

He moved up to the table occupied by Sheba, Apollo, Boomer and Bojay.

"It's good, what you're doing," he said. "We should all get acquainted. After all, we'll be fighting side by side from now on. Next round is on me."

The pilots from both ships applauded Cain, all save his daughter. She had heard that Cassiopea was aboard, but this was their first meeting since that time, yahrens ago, when the blonde socialator had usurped her mother's place.

"You'll have to excuse me," Sheba said, rising to her feet. "I think I've had enough combat for one day."

All eyes were on her as she left. There was a moment of awkward silence. Not everyone knew what had just transpired, but it didn't take much for them to see that there was clearly friction between the two women for some reason.

"Excuse me," Apollo said, getting up and going after Sheba.

"Nothing changes," Cassiopea said morosely.

"Everything changes," said Cain. "Come, let's have a drink for old times."

"Things may change," Cassiopea said softly, "but not people."

In the corridor, Apollo hurried to catch up to Sheba.

"Sheba, can we talk?"

"Not right now," she said. "I don't think I'm up to it."

"We're all going to have to work together if we're going to survive," he said.

"Working with you won't be the problem," she replied tersely.

"I don't think you understand," Apollo said. "We can't afford to have individual quarrels or rivalries. We're only human after all, and being human, we may have our differences, but we have a common enemy. And when it comes right down to it, there's not a person aboard the *Galactica* I wouldn't lay down my life for."

"Well, I'm sure that's very noble of you," Sheba said, a heavy touch of sarcasm in her voice. "However, I'm not so sure that everyone shares the purity of your motives. You can't know everyone as well as you seem to think you do."

"I know the lady you're upset about."

"Do you?"

"I know who she is now," said Apollo earnestly. "Who or what she may have been before doesn't count for anything. We've all been through a cleansing fire. It's stripped every one of us clean down to the bone. What's past is

47

past. We can afford to think of nothing but survival now. Only the strong survive."

"Not necessarily. Luck has a great deal to do with it. I know a little something about surviving, Captain."

"I know you think you do. But the fact is that it's easier in a cockpit with thrusters and lasers to defend you than it is for people in our fleet who have no choice but to sit and wait. And worry. I think you misunderstood me. It wasn't a warrior's strength that I was speaking of. Cassiopea is no warrior, but she's one of the people who work around the clock piecing together the wounded who aren't lucky enough to get out of the way. That doesn't take a warrior's skill, but it takes a great deal of courage."

"Cassiopea works in the Life Station?" Sheba said, obviously surprised.

Apollo smiled. "There's not much call for a woman of her old profession aboard the *Galactica*. Everyone's had to learn to contribute in some way. We're in this together, every one of us. Cassiopea has worked hard, harder than most, and she's become one of our best medics."

"All right, Apollo. Consider me briefed."

"What about convinced?"

"I'll be frank with you, Apollo, as one pilot to another. I don't convince easily. Human weakness is a given. It may lower its profile in a crisis, but it's still there."

She started to move off.

"What about you, Sheba?" he called after her. "Any weaknesses?"

She turned and regarded him with a steady gaze.

"None that will ever come between us, Captain."

Commanders Cain and Adama stood before the multi-dimensional war map in the ready room, going over their plan of battle with the squadron leaders looking on. Cain was giving them the final briefing.

"The Cylons run fuel ships along this route," he said, indicating the map. "They bring their tankers through every fifteen days. Their convoy will have already left Gomoray, but if we go full power all the way, we can still catch them before they're out of strike range."

"Full power all the way?" said Adama. He shook his head. "It's risky, Cain. You'll barely have enough fuel to get you there and back."

"We won't need any more than that," Cain replied with certainty.

"You'll still be playing it awfully close," Adama said. "Surely they must fly fighter escort on their convoys. A prolonged battle would use up all of your reserves."

"Except they'll never be expecting us to hit them," Cain said. "And besides, I don't fight prolonged battles with the Cylons. They're not that good. And *we* are!"

Adama frowned. Cain's bombastic rhetoric was having its desired effect upon the squadron leaders, it was psyching them up, but there was no denying the fact that his battle plan called for an extended strike that left absolutely no margin for error. They could not afford to lose any more ships. To say nothing of losing any more lives. Enough had died already. And there would be more before they reached their destination. It was inevitable. He was still the same old Cain. The man who lived for battle. That had never been Adama's way.

"Very well," Adama said, capitulating against his better judgment. They needed that fuel desperately and, risky though the plan was, it was nowhere near as dangerous as attacking the Cylon ground base would be. He would have to chose between the lesser of two evils. "We'll send a single squadron from each battlestar."

"No offense," said Cain, his glance taking in the squadron leaders from the *Galactica,* "but I'd prefer to use just my own wings on this mission."

"Commander, for purposes of morale, I think it would be best to begin integrating these squadrons so that they could start developing a sense of teamwork."

Cain shrugged. "Whatever you say. I'm sure my pilots will be more than happy to pass on their experience. Let's get to it."

Cain turned and left the ready room, his squadron leaders snapping to and following in his wake. Apollo stayed behind after the men from the *Galactica* had left, no doubt smarting a bit from Cain's remarks.

"Is there anything he doesn't do better than everyone else?" said Apollo.

Adama nodded. "I'd have to include giving up in that category."

"He isn't quite what I expected," said Apollo. "I've never seen anyone treated so like a . . . like a god."

"That may be," his father said, "but you have to remember that he's kept his people alive in the heart of Cylon territory for over two yahrens. They'd do anything for him. Rightfully so."

"I hope you realize," said Apollo, "that this . . . adulation, this absolute awe everyone feels for him in no way detracts from how the men feel about you."

Adama placed his hands on Apollo's shoulders.

"This isn't a popularity contest, son. It's a life and death struggle for survival. We need men like Cain. Our people need heroes. They need men and women whom they can look up to. People who can give them the courage to go on."

"They feel that way about you."

"And I hope I never disappoint them. Now get going. I don't want your squadron getting to those tankers after Cain's already done the job." He smiled. "There's a matter of pride involved here, understand?"

"Yes, sir."

As Apollo went off to do battle, Adama wondered about what he had told his son. A matter of pride. It was what Apollo wanted to hear. He felt the way any son might feel who saw his father overshadowed by another man. It was an understandable reaction, especially in one so young as Apollo.

He's a good warrior, Adama thought, but he has much to learn yet. When he gets older...if he ever gets that chance...he'll learn that there are times when one must swallow one's pride. He remembered back when Apollo had been a boy, the way he'd worshiped Cain. He would listen to the stories of Cain's victories and dream about the day when he too could be a warrior and command a battlestar. Now, as a man, Apollo was beginning to realize that even heroes have feet of clay.

Cain was a willful man, a man who did not know how to compromise. The men and women under his command, indeed, many of the people aboard the *Galactica,* felt about him the way Apollo had many yahrens ago. However, Apollo now realized the dangers inherent in hero worship. It was one thing to have respect for your commander, yet another to place him on a pedestal and pay him homage. To do that was to deny his humanity. Humans make mistakes, gods don't.

Adama knew that there would be no rest for him until the mission was successfully completed. They could not afford to make mistakes now.

• • •

There was a flurry of activity at the launch tubes of both battlestars as the strike wings prepared for launch. The launch crews of the Viper fighters hurriedly ran their systems checks and flight-suited pilots mounted the steps leading to the cockpits of their ships. Sitting in their cockpits, Boomer and Jolly started their engines, their faces calm and composed as they watched the indicator lights on their consoles. Through their helmet comcircuits, they heard the voices of their launch crews as they ran through the final checkpoints preparatory to flight. Apollo rested his hands lightly on the controls of his sleek fighter craft. He was in his element. His mind was in a state of meditative calm as he waited for the final countdown.

Aboard the *Pegasus*, a flight-suited Commander Cain strode confidently across the landing bay, heading for a Viper fighter. Sheba intercepted him.

"Father! What are you doing? I just found out you're going on this mission!"

"It's just a routine strike, Sheba. Nothing to it."

"Then why go?" she said, her face showing her concern. "We can't afford to risk losing you."

"I have to go, Sheba."

"But why?"

"Are you questioning my judgment, pilot?"

"No, sir, but—"

Cain's expression softened for a moment. "I'll explain later, Sheba. Don't worry. I know what I'm doing."

He turned and climbed into the cockpit of his Viper. Sheba wanted to protest, but he made it clear that there would be no questioning his decision. Besides, there was no time. She ran to her own Viper and vaulted into the cockpit. Within moments, she was hearing the voice of the launch officer through her helmet comcircuit.

"Transferring control to Silver Spar Squadron. Launch when ready."

Both Cain and Sheba fired their engines at the same time and their Viper fighters hurtled down the launch tubes and out into space.

CHAPTER FIVE

Athena glanced up from her screens to give the launch report to her commander.

"Blue Squadron launched and rendezvousing with Silver Spar Squadron from the *Pegasus,* sir."

Adama nodded at his daughter. He knew how much Athena would have liked to have gone on that mission. She was an accomplished Viper pilot, but he needed her on the command bridge. Besides, he already had one of his children risking his life out there. He had to admit to himself the very real possibility that he could lose Apollo. He couldn't bear losing both of them.

"It's kind of like the old days," said Colonel Tigh, standing by his side. "I mean the luxury of being able to divide the fighting load between two battlestars."

"Yes," said Adama. "It's a real blessing. And so was

finding Cain, with his knowledge of Cylon operations in this sector. Lord knows what would have happened if we'd stumbled into their territory."

"In a way, it's almost providential that we ran out of fuel."

The commander nodded. "Things do have a way of occurring in ways boggling to the mortal mind. Cain was a godsend."

"With all due respect," said Tigh, "I think that remains to be seen."

In the cockpit of his Viper, Boomer heard the voice of one of the pilots in the Silver Spar group coming through his comcircuit.

"Four centons to target . . ."

Boomer frowned. "Captain? Did that sound like . . . Cain?"

"Commander Cain," the reply came back at once. "And don't speak unless spoken to, Flight Sergeant . . . Boomer, isn't it?"

"Yes, sir, but—"

"I make it a point to know every man in my command," said Cain. "Three centons to target."

Apollo was perplexed. "Commander, I'm not picking up anything on my scanner. If we're only three centons to target—"

"You won't find them on your scanner, Captain," Cain replied.

"Then how—"

"I can *feel* them, Captain. I can feel them out there. Just ahead, you should be picking up a reading or our target convoy. Judging by the rate of speed of a full tanker and their departure time, we should be coming within scanner range of our target shortly. So this is where we split up, before they know we're out here."

"I thought we were going in as a single strike force," said Apollo.

"Captain, they'll have at least a dozen escort fighters to throw against us. We'll do this my way. Blue Squadron, head straight in, Silver Spar, follow me. . . ."

As Cain's squadron separated from the main body, Boomer's voice came through Apollo's comcircuit. The man sounded dubious.

"He's flying evasive tactics and we don't even have a target on our scanners," Boomer said.

"I somehow have the feeling he knows what he's doing," said Apollo. "Anyway, we'll know in a micron. If Cain's right, we should—"

At that moment, the target appeared on his scanner.

"There she is," Apollo said. "A Cylon tanker."

"I'll be a son of a ——"

"Make that two tankers," said Apollo, as a second image appeared on his scanner. However, the fact that he was reading their target meant that their target was also reading them. He now saw what Cain planned to do. He had sent Apollo's squadron straight in, into the Cylon's scanner range, while he would skirt their scanner range with his squadron, hitting them on their flank while they engaged Apollo. It was a sound strategy, but if he were late coming in. . . .

There was no sign of the fighter escort on his scanners. That made him worry. And then he saw them, racing out from behind the second tanker, coming in fast.

"Here we go," he said. "Let's take 'em, Blue. And for God's sake, whatever you do, don't hit those tankers!"

Blue Squadron came in hard and fast, the pilots peeling off from the formation at the last possible second. They were outnumbered four to one. As they engaged the Cylons,

Apollo had no time to wonder where Cain was. He had his hands full.

Almost at once, Boomer found himself with two ships on his tail. He fired at the ship ahead of him, missed, then used his thrusters to dart sideways at an angle, trying to get away from the laser fire that seemed to surround his cockpit in blinding light. He had to time it just right, waiting for his lasers to recycle, still it was impossible to be certain, for the two Cylon ships had not fired at the same time. He had only seconds in which to make his move and it could still wind up in his flying right into the path of one of their energy beams. He hit his thrusters and darted to one side, trying to get around behind the Cylons. His maneuver was successful, but one of their laser beams passed by so close that he was rattled for a moment and the Cylons were able to take advantage and recover.

Apollo successfully evaded the ships converging upon him only to see that Jolly was in trouble and he could not go to his rescue. It was all he could do to keep avoiding the laser fire that seemed to be coming from all around him.

"Roll, Jolly, he's on you!"

"I can't lose him, Apollo," Jolly's voice came back. "I'm in trouble!"

Suddenly, a blast of laser fire hit the Cylon fighter behind Jolly and the ship exploded into a silent fireball.

"Let's go get 'em!" Cain commanded, and to Apollo's immense relief, the Silver Spar Squadron joined the battle, taking the Cylons completely by surprise.

"Thanks, whoever that was," Apollo heard Jolly's voice say shakily.

"My pleasure," Cain replied. "Apollo . . . one your right wing!"

Apollo saw the Cylon coming in fast, angling in and firing.

"I've got him, Apollo," Sheba said, coming in almost on top of the Cylon and blowing him away.

Apollo took advantage of the reprieve to nail a Cylon fighter of his own. Cain's surprise attack had resulted in almost half the Cylon escort flight being destroyed as they were concentrating their attention on Blue Squadron. Before the Cylons could rally, Apollo, Boomer and Jolly had each scored hits of their own.

"They're running, Apollo!" Boomer shouted.

Apollo heard Cain's orders coming through instantly.

"Blue Squadron, two Cylon fighters peeling off and making a run for it—give pursuit."

Even as he spoke, Cain was zooming in on the nearest tanker. A slow-moving craft, it couldn't possibly escape the Vipers. Cain lined the tanker up in his sights and fired. The Cylon tanker exploded into a giant fireball and Cain powered his way through the blaze before it could dissipate, taking a dead heading on the second tanker.

Apollo closed with the sole remaining Cylon fighter. Its pilot wasn't even attempting to take evasive action. The Cylon was trying to outrun Apollo, but he was in range and it was an effort doomed to failure. Apollo had him in his sights. He thumbed the button that controlled his laser turrets and it was all over.

"That's all of them," he said. "Now let's go back and escort those tankers in. We need that fuel."

As he turned, Apollo saw Cain's fighter zooming down upon the tanker like a dreadnought. Cain fired. There were no tankers left to escort back to the fleet.

"Commander?" said Apollo.

Cain's voice sounded crisp and neutral over the comcircuit as he replied.

"Yes, what is it, Captain?"

"Were you aiming at a fighter? I didn't see him."

"You didn't, Captain? He was as clear as a Nubian Sun to me."

"What happened to the tankers?"

"I don't know. Looks like we've come up empty. Let's regroup the squadrons and head for home."

Apollo kept silent.

"Fighter squadrons returning, Commander," said Colonel Tigh.

Adama heaved a sigh of relief. The gamble had paid off. They were dangerously low on fuel.

"Only . . ." said Tigh, his voice trailing off.

"Only what, Colonel?"

"No tankers, sir. It appears they've been unable to locate the convoy."

Adama's heart sank. "Cain seemed so certain."

"What *is* certain is that we can't stay here, sir. We're too vulnerable. And we can't move without fuel. It looks like we have no options left. We're going to have to attack their main base."

Everything suddenly became crystal clear. Cain! Adama had refused to approve his plan to attack the Cylon ground base and now the commander of the *Pegasus* had forced his hand. Now they had no choice but to do it Cain's way.

"I want Commander Cain and the strike captains in my quarters as soon as they land," Adama said. He turned briskly and stalked off the bridge.

Tigh stood there tensely, watching the scanners as the strike force made its landing approach. He was old enough to remember Cain's battle tactics. The commander of the *Pegasus* was unquestionably a brilliant tactician and a superb flyer, but he had always been a maverick. A lesser man would have been broken for the things that Cain had done, only Cain had always brought results. This time the results could be disastrous. An attack on a Cylon ground base was dangerous enough in itself, but attempting to land there and steal their fuel? It was one thing to raid their convoys, as Cain had done to stay alive. But what he had now forced them to do seemed like certain suicide for whoever undertook the mission. Cain had set his plan in motion and now it could not be stopped. Indeed, thought Tigh, how do you stop a juggernaut?

Apollo stood in his father's private quarters, watching as Cain finessed his way out of taking blame for the destruction of the tankers. He was very smooth. The way he spoke, even Apollo might have believed him. But Apollo had been there and he knew what he had seen.

"I'm sorry, Adama," Cain was saying. "We were outnumbered and fighting for our lives. The fact that we came through it without casualties speaks well for our pilots, but still, with that many ships in combat, all around those tankers. . . ." He shook his head sadly. "I knew I was right when I suggested that we only send my squadrons. Nothing against Blue Squadron, but my people are more experienced in hit-and-run tactics against a convoy."

"You may be right," Adama said wearily. "Maybe it was a mistake to mix two forces that never fought together."

It was all Apollo could do to keep his temper in check. Cain was making it sound as though the tankers had been destroyed through sheer carelessness on the part of his strike wing.

"Commander," he said stiffly, "with all due respect, Blue Squadron was nowhere near those two tankers when they blew up. Commander Cain knows that perfectly well. It was on his order that we pursued and engaged the fleeing Cylon fighters."

Apollo looked directly at Cain as he spoke, challenging

the commander of the *Pegasus* to dispute him. Then he looked at Sheba, who could not have helped hearing her father's order to Apollo's squadron. She would not meet his gaze.

"Nothing personal, Apollo," Cain said. "You and your squadron handled yourselves as well as any warriors I've ever seen. It was a honor to have you along. And I wouldn't dream of attacking the Cylon ground base without you."

"You're not seriously suggesting that we—"

"I don't see that we have any choice now. Do you, Adama?"

"It does seem as though we have no other alternative," Adama said. His voice sounded strained. "I'll give you my decision later."

"It can't wait till later," said Cain. "We have to start working up a battle plan right now. I'd like—"

"I'll give you my decision."

"Adama, with all due respect—"

"Dismissed, Commander."

Cain stiffened. It was the first time Adama had pulled rank on him and it clearly didn't sit well. He started to say something in reply, then thought better of it. He nodded.

"Very well. I'll be in the Officers' Club. Let me know when you've made up your mind."

He snapped to and pivoted a smart about-face, departing without another word. The others followed him. No one seemed anxious to linger in that atmosphere of tension. No one except Apollo.

"Father..."

Adama turned to face him. Suddenly there was no point to saying anything. What Cain had done had locked them on their course. Cain's course. Adama had a difficult decision to make, the hardest part about it was that Cain had left him no alternatives. Like it or not, they would have to do it his way.

"Nothing," said Apollo and left the cabin.

Outside, he hurried to catch up to Cain and Sheba.

"Sheba..."

They stopped.

"I'd like to talk to you," he said.

Clearly, Sheba wasn't in a mood for having conversation. She had just seen her father effectively dressed down. Apollo wondered what else she had seen back on the strike mission.

"I was just about to join my father at the club," she said in a voice that indicated she wasn't anxious for Apollo's company.

"It's all right, baby," Cain said. "Talk to the man. Cassi and I will save you a place."

Sheba flinched slightly at the mention of Cassiopea's name.

"On the other hand, I think perhaps I'll skip the club and return to the *Pegasus*."

Cain nodded. "Suit yourself," he said and moved on.

Apollo stood in her way.

"Sheba, what happened out there?"

"You heard the report," she said stiffly. "The tankers were hit by incidental fire."

"Are you telling me that someone as good as you are, as good as the Silver Spar Squadron is, blew the whole purpose of our mission accidentally? Is that what you're saying?"

She hesitated. "That's what I'm saying."

Apollo's lips compressed into a thin line.

"Well. Then it appears we've found a weakness or two, haven't we, Lieutenant?"

She knew her father had purposely sabotaged the mission. There was no question in Apollo's mind, she knew. What galled Apollo was that she would not admit it. Angrily, he turned and left her before he could say something that later both of them might regret. As he had said to her before, they would have to work together. Only she had just made that a lot more difficult. Cain's words came back to him at that moment. "Like father, like daughter."

All the officers were gathered on the bridge of the *Galactica,* waiting to hear Adama's decision. They talked quietly amongst themselves. Only Cain was silent. He knew without a doubt what that decision was going to be. He had already made it for them. Adama entered and they all fell silent.

"Gentlemen, ladies," said Adama, nodding a curt greeting. "The data from the scanners aboard the *Pegasus* have made it clear that to attack the Cylon ground base on Gomoray would necessitate the forfeiture of countless lives. Those are losses unacceptable to me even if we were to successfully seize fuel from the Cylon depot."

"Adama," said Cain. "We have no choice. You know that as well as I do. Without fuel your fleet is dead. It's only a matter of time before the Cylon base ships arrive and attack us. They know we've destroyed their convoy. They know you're here, Adama."

"There is another alternative open to us," Adama said. "The *Pegasus* is carrying a maximum load of fuel. I'm going to divide it amongst the fleet."

"You'll *what?*"

"It will be sufficient to get us out of Cylon-controlled space with no loss of life. With any luck, we'll be able to locate another source of fuel before we run out."

"Commander," said Cain, "with all due respect, we cannot afford to risk the lives of every man, woman and child in the fleet on luck. All the fuel we need is right there at the base on Gomoray. By all that's holy, Adama, we have two battlestars to hit them with!"

"You seem to be forgetting one thing," Adama replied evenly. "Do you realize what could happen if we left this fleet of civilian ships unprotected while we went off to attempt conquering an entire planet?"

"We're not taking on the planet," Cain protested. "Our objective is the Cylon ground base. And we can do it, Adama. We can be in and out before they know what hit 'em."

"Cain, you know as well as I that we've been pursued by Cylon base ships ever since we left our own star system. They strike without warning. Even now, they could be closing in on us. You're asking me to gamble with the lives of everybody in my fleet."

"Anything is possible," said Cain. "I prefer to deal in probabilities, and the probabilities are that with our combined strength we can achieve our first clean victory since we lost the war. We can—"

"I'm not interested in victories," snapped Adama. "I'm interested in saving lives. The few lives we have left. Colonel Tigh, carry out the task of redistributing the fuel from the *Pegasus* throughout the fleet."

Cain's voice was icy as he spoke. "I will not allow that, Commander."

Adama's gaze locked with Cain's.

"You have no choice."

"I think I do. I think that two yahrens of surviving the Cylons with no help from you has earned my people the right to decide their own destiny."

"The way you decided the destiny of those Cylon tankers?" said Adama.

It was finally out in the open. There was no one aboard either battlestar who had not heard of the failure of the strike mission against the Cylon convoy. The silence on the bridge became a tangible thing.

"I did what I thought I had to do to assure the survival of our people," Cain said. "How long do you suppose the fuel supply from those two tankers would have lasted? We need enough fuel to sustain this fleet indefinitely. We *must* take that base."

"That's one opinion, Commander," said Adama. "It doesn't happen to be mine, and I'm going to alleviate your being forced into making any more decisions contrary to orders. As of this moment, you are dismissed from command. Colonel Tigh, you will assume command of the *Pegasus*."

Adama left the bridge. No one spoke. Slowly, all the officers began to file out. None of them looked at Cain, who stood stunned and alone.

Sheba and Bojay found Cain in the Officers' Club, sitting all by himself and drinking. Sheba had never seen her father looking so . . . defeated. They approached his table.

"Father," she said, "I want you to know that I, and the men, will follow you in whatever you decide to do."

Cain snorted. "Thanks, Sheba. But you heard the man. I don't decide anything anymore."

Bojay licked his lips nervously. "Sir, what we meant was—"

"I know what you meant. What I did on that strike mission was a matter of tactical misjudgment. Perhaps that's splitting hairs, but what you're thinking of is mutiny. I may be the most stubborn, egocentric warrior in the history of the colonies, but I'm also the *best* damned warrior in the history of the colonies. I have no intention of being remembered as the one who pulled out and left a lot of defenseless civilians at the mercy of the Cylons. Lord knows, I've always been . . . creative in interpreting the orders of my superiors, but there's no room for interpretation in Adama's relieving me of my command. He took the *Pegasus* away from me. In front of everyone. And there's nothing I can do about it."

Sheba fought to control the quaver in her voice. "He has no right. . . ."

"He has *every* right," said Cain. "Even if he were not on the Council of the Twelve, Adama's commission was posted before mine and he outranks me. It burns me, Sheba, but I'll not lead a mutiny. I may have had to live like a pirate for the past two yahrens, but I'll be damned if I'll *be* one."

Baltar had come a long way, in more ways than one. From a traitor condemned to death because he was of no further use to the Cylon Empire, he was now in command of three Cylon base ships. And he had come a very long way indeed, halfway across the galaxy, searching for the *Battlestar Galactica* and its pathetic fleet.

He had mixed emotions about his task. He wanted to see Adama dead more than he had ever wanted anything, and he knew that the Cylon leaders were not patient. Time and time again, Adama had eluded his grasp, and if he did not find and destroy the last survivors of the colonies soon, the Cylons might decide that his usefulness had ended. On the other hand, should he manage to destroy Adama's fleet, it was entirely possible that the Cylons would decide he was of no further use to them. They had set a human to catch a human, but at the same time they had sworn to exterminate humanity. Baltar was not convinced that he would be excluded. He already knew how well the Cylons kept their bargains.

Back when the Cylon Empire had sued for peace, there had been only two men who had not been taken in. Himself and Adama. Adama had sought to warn the Council of the Cylons' treachery, but they were all old men and weary of the war. They were willing to jump at any chance to bring the ages-old conflict to a close.

Baltar had not been fooled. He suspected that the Cylons were planning something underhanded, and rather than risk being destroyed with the rest of the old fools, he had approached the Cylons with an offer that fitted in perfectly with their designs. He would act as go-between for the Cylon Empire, lulling the Council into a false sense of security, thwarting Adama's efforts and buying the Cylon Empire the necessary time to enable them to get their base ships into position to launch an all-out strike against the colonies. In return for his services, the Cylons had promised to spare Baltar and his colony, to set him up as leader. They promised. As Baltar had seen it, there was no way for the colonies to win. He had no desire to die with them.

His efforts had helped the Cylons to make their victory a devastating one. But they had not spared his people. He could still recall the terror that he felt when he had been dragged from the presence of Imperious Leader by Cylon Centurions, screaming and begging for his life. If it had not been for Lucifer's intervention, he would have been beheaded and flushed out of the Cylon base ship with the garbage.

It all seemed so long ago. Baltar knew he was on borrowed time, but perhaps, just perhaps, he would be able to convince the Cylons that he was of more use to them alive than dead. Meanwhile they had allowed him all the privileges of a commander of a base ship, and he had every intention of enjoying his new station in life to its fullest extent.

Lucifer glided silently up to his throne.

"By your command," said the strange creation to whom Baltar owed his life.

"Speak."

"Our scouts have located the trailing vessels of the Colonial Fleet."

"They turned back before they were discovered, I trust," said Baltar.

"By your order," Lucifer replied.

"Well done. This is the final moment." Baltar sighed. "At long last I have overtaken Adama, with sufficient strength to wipe out the *Galactica* and its so-called fleet."

"It should be a good battle," Lucifer said.

"Battle." Baltar spat the word out. "It will be no battle at all. A single battlestar is no match for three base ships. What we have here, my dear Lucifer, is what is known as a rout...a humiliation...a massacre."

"Then you do not wish to send for support fighters from our base on Gomoray?"

Baltar smiled. "The only thing I want from Gomoray is a welcoming parade, a victory celebration, a tribute from the people of Gomoray to the greatest military leader the Cylon Empire has ever known. It cannot fail to impress Imperious Leader. I will convince him to let me have Gomoray as my seat of power, from which I will extend my dominion throughout the star system in the name of the Cylon Empire!"

"It might be wise," said Lucifer, "to first go through the formality of defeating the humans before ordering our victory celebration."

There were times when the sophisticated Cylon construct infuriated Baltar beyond all endurance. In spite of the fact that Lucifer had saved his life, Baltar hated the sentient machine. With its ability to tie into the base ship's computers, Lucifer had at his command more knowledge than Baltar could ever hope to amass, and Lucifer seemed to enjoy pointing out Baltar's shortcomings. Nevertheless, Baltar was the one whom Imperious Leader had placed in command, not Lucifer. A fact of which Baltar was fond of reminding Lucifer at every opportunity.

"That had a note of sarcasm, Lucifer," said Baltar. "Watch yourself. You are not the only I.L. series Cylon. You could easily be replaced."

"Forgive my impudence," said Lucifer, though he did not sound contrite. "Should I give the launch order?"

"Yes, yes, by all means," said Baltar, anxious now that the *Galactica* was within his grasp. "No . . . wait. I have an even better idea. I will accompany the strike force."

"You? Go into battle?" Lucifer modulated his voice to allow a much more subtle note of sarcasm to creep into it.

"Why not?" said Baltar. "Think of the impression it will create on the city of Gomoray when they learn that I personally led the final assault on the humans. Prepare a ship with your two best pilots."

"By your command," said Lucifer.

CHAPTER SIX

Apollo and Boomer brought the shuttle alongside the *Pegasus* and waited to receive their landing instructions. On the bridge, Colonel Tigh was at the command console, pacing nervously as Tolen manned the scanners.

"The fueling shuttles are coming alongside," said Tolen.

"Fine, bring them aboard and proceed with the redistribution of fuel to all the ships in the fleet," said Tigh.

It wasn't easy. Cain's crew clearly resented him. Tigh had dreamed, once, of commanding a battlestar, but not this way. Cain had brought it on himself. He had pushed too far. Still, it seemed that Adama had finally stopped the Juggernaut. That was how it seemed. Somehow, Tigh had his own doubts. Defeat was a word that was alien to Cain.

"Colonel?" said Tolen, seeming to read the thoughts going through his mind.

"Yes, what is it?"

"I think you know that there's a lot of bad feeling festering aboard this ship," Tolen said. "I wonder if we shouldn't delay this operation until things settle down a bit."

Tigh shook his head. He had his orders. They were firm and it was time to exercise his authority.

"Commander Adama wants the fleet to be able to get under way within a few centons," Tigh said. "We can't do that without fuel. Now carry out the order."

"Yes, sir."

Apollo gently eased the shuttle through the force field of the landing bay and set it down upon the deck. Jolly came up from the shuttle's cargo bay to announce that all was in order. Together, they climbed out of the shuttle only to be confronted by a dozen warriors led by Sheba and Bojay.

"Something we can do for you, Captain?" Sheba said.

"Not unless you want to assist in the transfer of fuel," Apollo replied.

"Oh?" said Bojay. "What transfer was that?"

Apollo was in no mood for games.

"We have a job to do," he said. "Stand aside."

None of the warriors moved.

"All right," Apollo said, glancing sideways at Starbuck. "What's going on here?"

"We're just standing up for our commander," Bojay said.

"Your commander accepted the order relieving him of command," Apollo said. "You would do well to follow his example."

"Look, Captain," Sheba spoke angrily, her tone of voice challenging Apollo to make an issue of it, "you don't seem to understand the situation. Adama humiliated my father, the greatest military man in the history of the colonies. A man who can think and fight circles around your father. He had no right to do that. It was an unconscionable act."

"She's right, Apollo," Bojay said. "Cain saved every one of us from certain death. Standing by him is the very least that we can do. You're not going to take that fuel."

"Look," Apollo said, anxious to avoid a confrontation; "no one wants to see Cain hurt or disgraced. That isn't—"

"It's a little late to be saying that, isn't it?" snapped Sheba.

"Don't you see, Commander Adama had no choice," said Boomer. "Cain left him none. He pushed Adama too far and there was only one course of action open to him. For better or for worse, there can only be one leader. What you people are doing constitutes mutiny."

"That's right," said Bojay. "You said that we can only have one leader, and the way we see it, we've got the wrong one. We fought for that fuel and we're going to keep it."

"I'm only going to say this once more," said Apollo tensely. "Adama is the fleet commander. He's determined that we're not going to send our defenses off on a wild gamble to take a Cylon ground base while the rest of the fleet is left helpless. I happen to support that thinking. So you'll either have to stand aside...or I'll blow you aside."

Before any of the warriors from the *Pegasus* could react, Apollo had his sidearm out, as did Boomer and Jolly.

"Well?" said Boomer. "What's it going to be?"

They never had the chance to find out. At that moment, the bridge sounded red alert throughout the ship.

"It's happened!" shouted Apollo, barely making himself heard over the din of the klaxon. "Just what my father was afraid of, we're under attack! Come on, Boomer, Jolly, we've got to get back to our ship!"

On the bridge of the *Pegasus,* Tigh suddenly found that the resentment of his crew was the least of his problems.

"Large Cylon task force coming in...."

"Fifty microns and closing...."

"Get me the *Galactica,*" snapped Tigh.

On the command bridge of the *Galactica,* there was an equal amount of pandemonium as the ship geared up for the attack.

"Forty-five microns and closing," Athena reported from her scanners.

"It's the largest task force since the destruction of Caprica," said Adama, his face grim. "They really mean to finish us this time."

Cain came charging onto the bridge.

"What is it?" he demanded. "What've they got?"

"We're not certain yet," Adama said, "but from the size of the attack fighter force on our scanners, I'd say they've got at least three base ships closing on us."

Cain stared at the scanner in disbelief. He swore, furious with himself.

"You were right, Adama. And I was wrong. Horribly wrong. If we had attacked their ground base, the fleet would have been completely at their mercy. Totally defenseless. I was a fool."

"It's no time for self-recriminations," said Adama. "What I need right now is your tactical wizardry. They didn't use much more than three base ships to wipe out our entire fleet at Caprica."

"Yes, but they had the advantage of surprise at Caprica," said Cain. "It might be on our side this time."

"Pull out the *Pegasus?*"

"Exactly. It's on the far side of the fleet and I doubt it's on their scanners yet. They don't know we've got *two* battlestars. I'll bring her around and squeeze them in between us. That is . . . if I've got my ship back?"

"Get going, Cain. And don't take too long getting into position. It's going to be awfully close."

"All right," said Cain, "but I'll be burning up a lot of fuel. I'll practically have to make light speed."

"Do I have a choice? You're going to have to burn off at least half your fuel to get around them, skirting their scanner range and still make it in time. Just be there when we need you."

"Twenty-five microns and closing," said Athena.

On board one of the Cylon fighters, Baltar relished the moment as his pilot gave the order to attack.

"This is going to be a classic defeat," said Baltar, licking his lips in anticipation. "It will be spoken of throughout the Cylon nation for the next thousand yahrens! Goodbye, *Galactica*. Goodbye, Adama. You're finished."

They weren't even making any effort to escape, thought Baltar. They knew it would be useless. The *Galactica*, possibly, would be able to outrun them, but that would mean leaving the rest of the fleet behind to be destroyed, and that fool Adama would never do that. They were going to stand and fight against overwhelming odds. They had no chance, none whatsoever. Baltar knew that he would get his victory and his place in the Cylon nation would be assured.

Starbuck was slammed back against his seat as he and every Viper aboard the *Galactica* launched to engage the Cylon task force. He felt the familiar surge of adrenaline as his Viper hurtled down the launch tube. He knew it was crazy. What sort of man would smile at the prospect of engaging an entire Cylon task force? Yet he was smiling. Gone from his mind were all thoughts of Cain and Cassiopea. Gone were all the questions that plagued him when he could not sleep. This was what he lived for. His heart seemed to slam against the inside of his chest as though it would break free at any moment to fall, pulsating wildly, upon the floor of the cockpit. All his senses seemed to be upon the verge of overload. Starbuck was feeling terror and it made him high.

"Okay, boys," he said to himself, "you want me, come and get me!"

On the bridge of the *Pegasus*, there was a flurry of activity as the crew ran for their battle stations.

"Incoming communication from Commander Cain, sir," Tolen said to Tigh. "Coming in on the scramble frequency."

"Put it on p.a.," said Tigh.

The image of Cain sitting in the cockpit of a Viper appeared on the monitors.

"I'm resuming command of the *Pegasus*, Colonel."

"So I've been informed by Commander Adama," said Tigh.

"Good. Now get that ship out of there. Swing her around in a one-eighty and head out on course one one oh. Stay out of the Cylons' scanner range. I'll rendezvous with you."

"What about the attack force coming in?"

"You let me worry about that. Have all fighters standing by, ready to launch. I'll be aboard in ten minutes. Cain out."

A cheer went up from every man and woman on the bridge. Tolen, swept up in the spirit of the moment, turned to Tigh and tried, unsuccessfully, to wipe the smile from his face.

"Nothing personal, Colonel" he said. "It's just that—"

"I quite understand," said Tigh. "After all, who can fight a living legend?"

Every monitor aboard the *Galactica* showed the Cylon fighters streaking in to the attack. Athena counted off the time to contact.

"Closing fast . . . ten . . . nine . . . eight . . . seven . . . six . . . five . . . four . . . three . . . two . . . one. . . ."

"Positive shield," said Adama.

The shield slid over the massive observation port on the bridge as the Cylons attacked. Every monitor showed Cylon fighters and Vipers engaging.

Baltar kept his fighter out of the fray, at a safe distance from which he could observe the battle.

"This time the *Galactica* doesn't have a chance," he said. He was in communication with Lucifer, aboard his base ship. "Concentrate our fighters on the *Galactica*'s landing bays. Destroy them and her warriors won't be able to land to refuel."

The Cylon fighters converged on the landing bays and scored several telling hits.

"Fire in the bay," reported Omega, "deck three."

"Damage control," snapped Adama, "how bad is it?"

"It's out of control, sir. We're going to have to shut off Alpha bay and turn off the force field."

"They're using our own tactics against us for a change," Adama said. "Destroy our ability to land our fighters and then run them out of fuel. Not that we have any to give them."

"Baltar?" said Omega.

Adama nodded. "Of course."

"I'd say they were in for a slight surprise," Omega said.

I hope so, thought Adama. *Cain! Where are you?*

"Continue leading her warriors away from the fleet," said Baltar. "They can't keep using full power on their thrusters for very long."

"A word of caution," Lucifer's voice came back to him over his comcircuit. "We, too, are expending great amounts of fuel in a sustained attack."

"Yes, but our fighters have a place to land and theirs do not. Or will not before long."

"We have always found it best to attack and then fall back," said Lucifer.

"That's why you always lose," Baltar replied. "We have the last surviving battlestar just about ready for the kill. There will be no falling back. Not this time. This time we finish it!"

Aboard the *Pegasus,* Cain was once more in command, having practically burned up his Viper's engines in order to effect the rendezvous.

"Steady . . . steady, skirt their scanner range as closely as possible. We can't give our position away. Not yet."

"We are now running parallel to the attacking Cylons on their rear flank," reported Tolen, "but the *Galactica* is taking some pretty heavy damage."

"Helm, stand by. . . . We're going in."

Baltar exalted as he watched the *Galactica* take hit after hit. Her shields couldn't hold up much longer. They had extinguished the fires in her landing bays by sealing them off and shutting down the force fields, allowing the air inside to escape, but that also effectively neutralized those bays, since the ground crews would not be able to enter them without their suits, and the attacking fighters would now easily fire directly through the massive entry ports, causing even more damage. Baltar watched as the Vipers tried in vain to intercept the Cylon craft as they made their passes at the *Galactica*. He had to give Adama's people their due, they were putting up a valiant resistance, but they were too outnumbered.

"Sir, if I may—"

"Not now," said Baltar, cutting off one of his Cylon pilots. "I don't want to miss a moment of the last battlestar's destruction."

"What about the other battlestar?" the pilot asked.

"What are you babbling about? *What* other battle . . ." Baltar's voice trailed off as the scanner on his fighter craft picked up the *Pegasus* closing with them fast.

"It's *impossible*," he said.

"No, sir. It is a second battlestar and it is closing with us at the rate of—"

"Turn, you fool, turn! He's coming straight for us!"

Like seeds exploding from a pod, the Vipers from the *Pegasus* launched from their mother ship and attacked the task force. Baltar panicked.

"Retreat! Order the retreat! Return to our base ships!"

"But the *Galactica*—"

"Our fighters are half out of fuel and those Vipers are coming in fresh," said Baltar. "Now do as I say before they cut us off!"

Tolen looked up from his monitor screens on the bridge of the *Pegasus*. The plan had worked.

"The Cylon fighters are retreating, sir."

"Go after them," said Cain. "Get as many as you can before they reach their base ships. Then bring your warriors home."

Cain turned to his communications officer.

"Get me the *Galactica*."

There was not a moment of rest for Adama as he coordinated the defensive squadrons and directed the damage control teams in their work.

"What's the situation with the sealed-off landing bays?" he asked.

"Heavy damage, sir, but not insurmountable," said Omega, his face showing the strain. "We're working on the force field generators and clearing away some of the wreckage, but they've breached our hull in several places and it'll be quite some time before we can effect repairs and land any of our Vipers."

"Thank God the *Pegasus* is with us or we'd lose every ship," said Adama.

"Commander Cain on the line," said Athena.

"Adama? You alive?"

"I appear to be," Adama replied. "Thanks for the assist. It wasn't looking too good for a while there."

"It doesn't look too good now," said Cain. "What's your status?"

"Everything is under control for the moment," said Adama. "I've got my people running themselves ragged trying to repair the damage, but I'd like you to land some of our fighters. It's going to take some time to repair all our landing bays."

"My pleasure," said Cain. "Commander, may I suggest we call a council of war as soon as possible? Those Cylons are in a state of shock right now, but that won't last long."

"I agree," Adama said. "We'll meet in twenty centons in my quarters."

"I'll be there," said Cain.

CHAPTER SEVEN

It was dark inside the war room. The only illumination came from the giant star map before which stood Adama, Cain, Apollo, Tigh and Tolen. In the shadowed silence of the war room, it was almost possible to forget the frenzied activity that went on throughout the rest of the *Galactica* as her crew worked desperately to allow the ship to recover from the devastating attack of the Cylon task force. Each of the men inside the war room knew that the battlestar could not withstand another such attack.

"It's confirmed," Apollo said. "They've got three base ships."

"Plus whatever they want to throw at us from Gomoray base," said Cain.

Tigh shook his head. "We can't allow them to launch that united assault. We'd never survive."

"We've got to knock out that ground base on Gomoray and we've got to do it *now*," said Cain.

Adama knew that, even with the *Pegasus*, they would not be able to fight against an assault from both the ground base and the base ships, still, to go on to the offensive when the odds were so heavily against them seemed insane. But then, everything about the rag-tag fleet was insane. Those ships had never been designed for deep-space travel and yet they had come this far. The odds against their ever finding Earth were also incredible, but that was what they had set out to do. How much longer, Adama wondered, can we get away with pushing our luck?

"We've got to do it, Adama," said Cain, seeing the commander of the *Galactica* hesitating. "It would take them completely by surprise. We've got a chance and we've got to take it. It's the only way."

"He is right about that, Father," said Apollo. He knew that it was no longer a case of leaving the fleet defenseless to mount an unnecessary attack on Gomoray. If Gomoray joined the base ships in their next attack, nothing they could do would enable them to defend the fleet, much less themselves.

"Spending lives in exchange for that ground base is against everything I believe in," said Adama. "Is there no other choice available to us?"

"Adama," Cain said, "two battlestars can overwhelm Gomoray. We won't suffer any losses."

Apollo shook his head. "With all due respect, sir, I can't agree with you on that. Cylon anti-aircraft batteries are practically foolproof. We could never hope to get past them without sustaining casualties."

"Yes, if we went in in force," said Cain. "But we could send in a small team to neutralize their anti-aircraft batteries. Then our Viper squadrons could sweep over the city and shut down the whole place. Then we go in and keep on fighting until Gomoray is ours."

"No," said Adama. "We cannot attempt to capture a land base. The only thing we can hope to gain from Gomoray is the fuel we need to elude those base stars."

"As soon as they discover what we've done," said Apollo, "they'll send those base ships against us with everything they've got. Our fuel landing teams would be vulnerable targets on the ground—they'd never lift off."

"Once we secure the fuel base," said Cain, "I propose we withdraw one battlestar to delay those incoming base ships."

"A single battlestar to fight off three Cylon base ships?" said Adama.

"Not fight off, old friend. Delay. I'll give the impression that we're leaving Gomoray. I'll lead them away."

"You seem to have decided that it's to be the *Pegasus* that withdraws and tackles the base ships," said Adama.

Cain shrugged. "The *Galactica* is damaged."

"What about the ground force?" said Adama. "We have no intelligence reports on the installation."

"Some of my fighters have flown so close to it that by now they probably know the name of every Cylon down there," Cain replied.

"Father, if this installation is anything like the one on Naytar, Starbuck and I have already taken one apart. All we'd have to do is get inside."

Adama turned away from them and walked across the war room. As the ranking officer, he would have to make the final decision. And he would have given anything not to have to make it. He couldn't leave it up to Cain. The commander of the *Pegasus* was a good officer, but he took too many risks. He had earned his nickname, the Juggernaut had. Once Cain made up his mind, he went ahead at all costs, with winning as his only objective. Adama could not fault him for that, but he could not afford Cain's tactics in this case. There were so few of them left, he thought. Human life was precious. To take a chance on losing even one seemed unthinkable, yet how was it possible to mount a military operation with no loss of life? Especially an operation such as the one that Cain was proposing.

He was right about one thing, though, and Apollo had seen that, as had the others. It would be impossible for the fleet to survive a unified attack from the base ships and the ground base on Gomoray. In a way, they had Baltar to thank for the fact that they had survived the attack of the three base ships. Baltar could have summoned up an attack force from Gomoray, but he had not known about the *Pegasus* and he had thought, correctly, that his force alone was enough to destroy the *Galactica* and its fleet of defenseless ships. Had he been concerned only with achieving his objective, he might have been more thorough and called the ground base for assistance, but Baltar wanted glory. Adama knew him well. He wanted to impress his Cylon superiors. Now that he knew he was going up against not one, but two battlestars, Baltar would doubtless muster as large a force as he could. Even now, they were probably regrouping and preparing their battle plan, making ready for another attack. This time, Adama knew, they would not have the advantage of surprise. This time, the Cylons would be ready for them and they would not retreat.

He turned back to Cain.

"I'd like to see you in my quarters, Commander."

There was no time for small talk. Cain got right to the point.

"Look, Adama, if you're worried about a repetition of that tanker incident—"

"That's precisely what I *am* worried about," said Adama heatedly. "I'm a great admirer of your strategic genius, Cain, but yours is a history of individual initiative. Not teamwork. I'm not sure you really understand our problem. We're not at war with the Cylons anymore, not in the sense you seem to think we are. That war is over and we lost. I'm not concerned with winning military victories, Cain, I don't care about Gomoray beyond getting the fuel we so desperately need. I'm fighting a war of *survival*."

Cain sighed. "Adama, I can't lie to you. I want to win. Just surviving isn't enough for me. Nothing would please me more than taking Gomoray and running up our flag, but I know now that's impossible."

"Do you? Do you fully comprehend the liability of having to fight a military campaign while protecting a fleet of one hundred and twenty civilian ships?"

"Adama, believe me, I know how you feel. I know what you're up against and have been up against ever since you left Caprica burning behind you. I know it couldn't have been easy. I don't want to make it any more difficult for you. The very heart of my plan is to use the *Pegasus* to divert those base ships away from you, to give you the chance to return to the fleet with enough fuel to put you safely out of their range."

"I appreciate your good intentions," said Adama. "I just don't want any more surprises. I can't afford them."

"Then the mission is a go?"

"I don't really have any choice, do I?"

"No, old friend. I'm afraid you really don't."

"I only know that you'll be taking an incredible chance," said Adama. "And that if you fail, it will be all over for us."

"I won't fail."

"I hope you know what you're doing."

"I believe in what I'm doing," said Cain.

"That's not the same thing," Adama said.

"Perhaps not. But it's all I've got. It's all you've got, too."

"Yes," said Adama, "I'm afraid so. Good luck, Cain."

"And to you."

Cain left the room. Outside, Tolen and his two aides fell in step with him. They moved briskly, heading toward the *Galactica*'s one fully operational landing bay. Cain heard the sound of running footsteps and turned to see Cassiopea catching up to them. She was out of breath.

"Cain . . . what is it? What's happening? I just heard you were returning to the *Pegasus*."

"That's right."

"I was hoping we could talk . . ."

"And I was hoping you'd say that, Cassi. But this just isn't the time. I'm sorry."

"I could ride over to the *Pegasus* in your shuttle."

"I'm afraid not. It'll be safer for you here. Besides, I don't think they can spare you."

"Safer?" Cassiopea's eyes grew wide with alarm. "Why? What are you planning to do?"

"It's a mission, Cassi. Nothing we can't handle, but it's no place for civilians."

"Who's a civilian? We're all fighting for our lives. You must need more medical techs aboard the *Pegasus*. Take me with you."

"Cassi. . . . You'll understand later. Just trust me. Please."

Cain leaned forward and kissed her lightly on the lips.

"Commander," Tolen said uneasily.

"Yes, right away. Cassi, I'll be back. You know that. Try to spend some time with Sheba."

"How can I?" said Cassiopea miserably. "She hates me."

"Try. I love you, Cassi."

He turned and hurried away with his party, without looking back.

Cassiopea wanted to run after him, but she knew it would be pointless. There was nothing she could say, nothing she could do that would deter him from whatever it was he had decided upon. That was how Cain was. But there had been a time when she had known another Cain, one very different from the man whom everyone called "the living legend."

It had not been all that long ago, but it seemed to Cassiopea that she had lived a lifetime since then. So much had happened since that time when an eighteen-year-old socialator had met a broken man in a tavern on Caprica.

She had not known then, when they first met, that he was the celebrated Commander Cain of the *Battlestar Pegasus*. All she knew was that he was a man in a great deal of pain.

He was sitting all by himself in a shadowed corner, his hands cupped around a goblet of baharri, but he seemed to have forgotten all about his drink. He didn't seem to be at all aware of his surroundings. He sat very straight and very rigid, eyes staring but not seeing anything. At first she thought that he was drunk and would have passed him by, but then she saw how clear his eyes were. She stood right in front of him, but he hadn't seen her. He seemed to be looking inward, at something that was torturing him. Tears were flowing down his cheeks. Cautiously, she had moved closer, then sat down beside him.

"Are you all right?" she had asked him.

He had not replied. Gently, she placed her hand on his right forearm. He turned toward her, eyes focusing upon her face. She saw a momentary flicker of surprise, then puzzlement.

"I beg your pardon?" he had said. His voice seemed perfectly calm and controlled.

"I asked you if you were all right."

"Oh. Why, yes, I'm fine." He frowned slightly. "Why do you ask?"

"Well..." she hesitated. "For one thing, you're crying."

He raised his hand to his face and felt the tears. He swallowed and looked down at his hands, still cupping the goblet.

"I was not aware of it," he said softly.

"Perhaps if you talked about it?" she suggested.

He wiped his eyes.

"No. No, I don't think so. Thank you just the same, though."

He placed some bills on the table and slid them toward her. She looked down at them, then back at him. She didn't say anything and made no move to take the money.

"I–I'm dreadfully sorry," he stammered. "I seem to have made an embarrassing mistake. I thought you were..." He decided not to compound the mistake any further.

"What if I am?" she said.

"I'm afraid I don't understand."

"I did not ask you for money. Whatever it is you're feeling, I don't think you could buy your way free of it."

The corners of his mouth twitched slightly. "No, you're right there."

He took the money back.

"You know, sometimes it helps to talk to a total stranger," Cassiopea said. "It's not like burdening a friend with your troubles. And I'm a very good listener."

He remained silent.

"What have you got to lose?" said Cassiopea.

"That's true," said Cain. "I've already lost everything."

He began to open up to her, hesitantly at first, and then it all came bursting forth in a torrent of emotion. He had been off on a military campaign and while he had been gone his wife had taken ill and died. He was a dedicated soldier and, as such, had little time to spend at home with his family. He had lived for the day when the war with the Cylons would finally be over and he would be able to return to Caprica, to his family, and now his wife, the only woman he had ever loved, was gone. Her love had been what kept him going and without her he was shattered. As he spoke, the tears began to flow again and soon he was sobbing openly, unashamedly. Cassiopea could tell that he was not a man who cried easily.

They did not become lovers, not at first. What Cain needed was a friend, someone he could talk to and lean on for support, and Cassiopea was happy to provide that for him. They saw each other often; they would talk late into the night, sharing their experiences with each other. Many times, they would get together at his home and it was there that Cassiopea met Sheba for the first time.

They were about the same age and, from the holographic projections Cain had shown her, Cassiopea could see how much Sheba resembled her mother. Even then, at that young age, Cassiopea had understood why Cain was unable to share with Sheba what he shared with her. Sheba was the image of her mother and a constant reminder to Cain of the woman he had loved and lost. He blamed himself for his wife's death, even though the doctors had told him that there was nothing that he could have done. The disease had been without a cure. Still, Cain felt an enormous amount of guilt over the fact that he had not been with her when she died and, as a result, he found it very difficult to spend much time with his daughter. He understood the situation, but time had not yet healed his wound enough for him to overcome it and he blamed himself for failing Sheba, as well.

Sheba idolized her father and, though she could share

his grief, she felt frustration at not being able to help him. This frustration grew into resentment. She resented Cassiopea for being able to give her father something she could not, and she was angry at her for taking her father away. This anger turned to hatred when, after a time, Cain and Cassiopea became lovers.

Cain changed after a time or, rather, he became his old self once again. When he was called back to duty, the best therapy in the world for him, he once again became the iron-willed commander of the *Pegasus* and, though they still shared their special closeness, Cassiopea was never again to see his vulnerability. For a short while, Cain had shown Cassiopea his inner self. She had helped him to pull himself back together once again and, when they parted, it was with the understanding that he would return to her and then they would see where their relationship would lead. While he was gone, having taken his daughter with him to train as a cadet, Cassiopea went about her daily life, dreaming of the day he would return and hoping that she would find a way to overcome Sheba's ill feeling for her. Then she heard that they had perished at the Battle of Molecay.

Back then, she had thought the world had ended. She never suspected that her world would literally end when the Cylons attacked the colonies and wiped them out. She had been lucky to survive and luckier still to find a berth aboard the *Galactica*. When she met Starbuck for the first time, she had been attracted to him and it had not been until much later that she realized how much of the attraction had been due to the fact that, in many ways, he reminded her of Cain. The two men were different, but she imagined that when Cain had been much younger, he must have been very much like Starbuck. They both possessed forceful, dynamic personalities, a great deal of energy, and both were brash, prone to taking risks. Now she felt herself torn between them and she did not know what to do.

Starbuck had been very understanding. He had not pressured her to choose and, although he tried not to show his jealousy, she knew he must have felt it. Then, too, there was a vulnerability in Starbuck that he kept hidden, just like Cain. It didn't make matters any easier that they were all in a great deal of danger. She loved two men and either one or both of them could die within the next few centons. In a way, Cassiopea envied them. They only had to fight one war.

The bridge of the *Galactica* was as busy as it would be during a red alert. Athena and Omega manned their consoles, taking reports from damage control and co-ordinating efforts to secure needed raw material from the other ships in the dilapidated fleet. Fortunately, the Cylons had concentrated their attack on the battlestar, hoping to destroy their greatest threat first so that they could then dispose of the remainder of the fleet at their leisure. Thanks to the *Pegasus,* the fleet had escaped damage from the Cylon attack, with only a few ships taking hits from incidental fire. Only those most severely damaged would be scavenged for material to repair the *Galactica*. Accommodations would become even more crowded, but no one would complain. They were happy to have survived.

"Commander Cain has just departed for the *Pegasus,* sir," said Colonel Tigh.

Adama nodded thoughtfully. "I wonder if we'll ever see him again," he said quietly.

Tigh frowned. "But I thought you felt his plan was sound."

"It was the only plan we had," replied Adama. "I'd give

anything to have an alternative."

"But you're sending Apollo with the ground assault team," said Tigh.

"Yes," Adama said. "I am."

He sat down in his chair, leaned back and closed his eyes. Tigh did not envy him. He had had a brief taste of what it was like to command a battlestar and, brief though it had been, it had been enough. Perhaps Cain got all the glory, Tigh thought, but Adama was the real hero. It was a role he never wanted, but he had accepted it because there had been no one else. If they managed to find Earth, Adama would be hailed as a savior, but at that moment, Tigh knew that he would trade it all just to get a night of peaceful sleep.

CHAPTER EIGHT

Boomer glanced up at Apollo as he strapped on his laser holster. They were in the pilots' ready room, gathering together the gear that they would need for their infiltration mission.

"Look," said Boomer, licking his lips nervously, "what are our chances of coming out of this thing? I mean, it sounds crazy. Walking right into a Cylon city. . . . What do you think the odds are?"

"You really want to know?" Apollo said.

Boomer snorted. "Yeah. That's what I thought."

Apollo's face was grim. "You want to back out? No one will blame you if you do."

Boomer straightened up and put his hand on Apollo's shoulder.

"Hey, friend—where you go, I go. Okay?"

Starbuck entered the ready room, carrying a large equipment bag. From it he withdrew several extra laser pistols and handed them to Boomer and Apollo.

"I checked out a little extra firepower for this mission," Starbuck said. "I figured we would need it."

"Sounds really encouraging," said Boomer, strapping the other pistol onto his opposite side, so that he could use one in either hand if need be.

"This where we report in for the mission?" said Bojay, entering with Sheba.

"What do you mean?" asked Apollo.

"We've been assigned to the *Galactica* ground force."

"By whose orders?" said Apollo.

"My father's," Sheba said. She dropped her equipment bag on the floor and started to get into her jump suit. "We are, after all, the only people in this room familiar with the target. It would help to have some idea where you're going, wouldn't it, Captain?"

"You've *been* there? On the ground?"

"No," said Sheba, "but we've been over it many times in our hit-and-run missions on the ground base. Since we'll be making free-flight jumps, it won't be that much different. I'll know just where to bring us down."

"No reflection on your abilities," said Apollo, "but I'm just a little puzzled. It doesn't sound like your father, risking you on a..." he hesitated.

"One-way mission?" Sheba said.

Starbuck cleared his throat. "Ah, look lady, no offense, but this kid doesn't go on one-way missions. And I don't take too kindly to heroes who start out planning on not coming back."

"Sorry," Sheba said. "I'm just being a realist."

"If we were realists, we'd all be dead back on Caprica," said Starbuck. "Where's our medical tech? I want to get going before I start to get the jitters."

"We're not taking one," said Sheba.

"What?"

"I said, we're not taking one. We won't have time to stop for wounded. We're going to have to get in and out as fast as possible."

Starbuck forced a smile. "Okay. That's all right, too. My kind of mission . . . short."

"You're an optimist," said Sheba.

"Like to make a little side bet that we make it?" Starbuck asked.

Their eyes met.

"What's the side bet?" Sheba asked.

"Oh, why don't we make it something real personal?" said Starbuck, his eyes not leaving hers.

Sheba's lips curved up in a half smile. "Bad idea, Lieutenant. You wouldn't want me to throw the mission just to avoid paying up, would you?"

She finished fastening the closures on her jump suit and left along with Bojay.

"Interesting lady," Starbuck said.

Boomer shook his head in disbelief.

"You're something else, Starbuck," he said. "You can think of sex at a time like this?"

"Later on, I may not have the time," said Starbuck. "Besides, the way my luck's been running, she probably *will* throw the mission just to frustrate me."

Apollo grinned. "Starbuck? Frustrated?"

"Yeah. Remember, you heard it here first."

They suited up and picked up the remainder of their gear. Together, they headed for the elevator that would take them down to the landing bays. They all remained silent on the way down, each keeping his thoughts to himself. The odds were heavily against them. And there was no comfort to be derived from the knowledge that if they didn't make it, chances were that no one else would either. As they stepped off the elevator, Cassiopea was waiting for them.

"Starbuck, I have to talk to you."

"You picked a great time," he said. "We're ready to launch."

"That's what I want to talk to you about. I know about your jump. Where are they sending Cain?"

"I'm about to jump into an inferno and you want to talk to me about Cain? That's just great."

"You don't understand," she said, grabbing his arm to restrain him. "Cain isn't planning on coming back."

"Starbuck!" Apollo called him from the shuttle's hatch. "Come on, let's move!"

"Look, Cassi," Starbuck said, disengaging himself and walking quickly toward the shuttle, "Cain's a survivor. He'll be back, if that's what's worrying you."

Cassiopea kept pace with him.

"If Cain was expecting to come back, he would have let me come aboard the *Pegasus*," she said.

Sheba threw her gear bag into the shuttle and turned at the sound of their approach. "What are you talking about?" she said, having heard Cassiopea's last comment.

"Nothing," said Apollo. "We're all in the same fix. The odds are against us, but we'll get through. We have to."

"No," said Sheba. "She's right. If my father left her off his ship, he has to be planning something crazy. I've got to get back to the *Pegasus*."

Apollo held her back.

"Sorry. You're with us, for better or for worse. Your father's orders, remember?"

"I lied," she said. "He doesn't know anything about it. It was my own idea."

"I'll take her place," said Cassiopea.

"Are you crazy?" Starbuck said.

Apollo's reaction was more to the point. "You can't get us to our objective on the Gomoray ground base," he said. "She can."

"What about your medical tech?" said Cassiopea. "I don't see one."

"We don't have one."

"You do now." She pushed past him and entered the shuttle.

"Cassiopea. . . . Oh, for—"

"Apollo," said Boomer, "come on. We're microns from launch."

Cassiopea sat down in the shuttle next to Starbuck.

"Where do you think *you're* going?" he said.

"On the mission."

"Dressed like that? This is a jump."

She pointed to the equipment bag she had placed in the shuttle moments before the others had arrived at the landing bay.

"Everything I need is right here." She opened the bag, pulled out a jump suit and started to get into it.

"No way," said Sheba. "I'm not going to allow her to come along. I don't even want her on the same shuttle with me."

"It's too late," said Apollo. "We're about to launch. Besides, it's not up to you. She's one of us."

"Nice tight-knit team we have here," grumbled Boomer.

"Yeah," Starbuck replied. "With support troops like this, who needs Cylons?"

"Shuttle stand by to launch." Tigh's voice came over the comcircuit.

In the background they could hear Adama's voice, not quite out of mike range, giving the order to launch. Tigh repeated it and, as they left the *Galactica*'s landing bay, they heard Adama's voice again, just off mike.

"May the Lord be with you," Adama said.

Lucifer glided up to the clear doors of the throne room of the Cylon flagship. His red glowing optical sensors picked up the shape of Baltar, sitting on the throne and brooding. Lucifer could have opened the doors by reaching out and pressing the plate set into the wall, but it was easier and quicker to use his remote tie-in to the ship's computer, an extension of his extremely complex brain. The doors slid open and Lucifer rolled forward on his silent tracks, stopping just in front of the throne.

"Baltar..."

The human turned around to face him. He was angry at being disturbed.

"What is it?"

"We must talk," said Lucifer, adjusting his vocal mechanisms to produce a subtle, deferential tone.

"Not now."

"Time is of the essence, Baltar. I am sorry that your victory did not work out quite the way you planned—"

"Get out of here!"

"Baltar, even the Imperious Leader in one of his most difficult moods could hardly blame you for running from two battlestars."

"I did *not* run," said Baltar through gritted teeth. "I executed a tactical retreat, you imbecile."

"There is no reason to be abusive," said Lucifer, anxious to reason with his superior. "You forget, I am on your side. I have placed my fate into your hands. My rise to a position of supremacy over my fellow I.L. series Cylons is completely dependent on your success. Or lack thereof."

"Spare me," said Baltar wearily. "What is the latest intelligence? As if I should put any faith in scanners that cannot report the presence of two battlestars rather than one."

"It is the consensus of the commanders aboard the two supporting base ships that we should summon aid from the base at Gomoray at once," said Lucifer.

"Oh, it is, is it?"

"It would seem to be a prudent idea," Lucifer said. "Had you something else in mind?"

Baltar grimaced. "I somehow find the idea of some base commander on Gomoray taking credit for destroying the *Galactica* slightly annoying. Especially since we've come so far and are now poised for the kill."

"We already had one opportunity to destroy the fleet of the escaping humans and we did not do so well," said Lucifer.

Baltar slammed his fist down onto the arm of his throne.

"We were taken by surprise! Thanks to your so-called intelligence reports. How many squadrons are based on Gomoray? Or is the Cylon strength in the area also a mystery to you?"

"I can tell you precisely what we can expect in the way of support from Gomoray," said Lucifer. "Four full squadrons. The equivalent of a base ship."

"In other words, we have the firepower of four base ships at our disposal?"

"Exactly."

"How long would it take to bring them into action? In an emergency?"

"It would depend to a great extent upon their battle readiness and the efficiency of the base personnel and their commander," Lucifer replied. "I would not advise waiting too long."

Baltar considered the suggestion. "If we caught the *Galactica* and her support ship between the two forces, there would be no question of victory."

"That is the opinion of our support commanders."

"Very well," said Baltar. "Prepare our ships for another attack."

"Notify all ship captains that the *Galactica* and *Pegasus* are moving off, leaving them temporarily unguarded," said Adama, the battlestar prepared to get under way.

"That's not going to make them happy," Tigh said. "Do we tell them any more than that?"

Adama shook his head. "I don't think that will be necessary. If we stay here and those two forces hit us, we won't be any help to them. I think they realize that. But use code. Let's not tell the Cylons that we're coming. Helm, make ready to get under way. Flank speed, fuel be damned. If those base ships launch a new attack, we're not going to need it anyway. We won't be going anywhere."

Aboard the bridge of the *Pegasus,* Tolen kept Cain posted on the progress of the other elements of their mission.

"The shuttle with the ground force has reached Gomoray air space," he said. "The *Galactica* is under way."

"Then this is it," said Cain. "All warriors to battle stations."

The klaxon sounded red alert over the p.a. system of the *Pegasus*.

"Helm, full speed for those base ships."

"Yes, sir," Tolen replied nervously. Cain had never let them down before, but then he had never set off against three Cylon base ships singlehanded.

"*Pegasus* is under way," Athena said from the command console on the bridge of the *Galactica*.

Adama took a deep breath. "My heart is with those four young warriors over Gomoray," he said. "They've got the roughest part of it. And if they fail, then it's all over—for them and for us."

"They should be nearing their drop zone about now," said Tigh.

"Yes. A drop right into the heart of a Cylon capital. How did we ever get this desperate?"

Aboard the shuttle, as it neared the drop point, the cockpits lights shifted from a dim white to red and a small buzzer began to sound intermittently.

"This is it," Apollo said.

They stood and moved toward the hatch, awaiting the command of their shuttle pilot. Omega glanced back at them.

"Stand by," he said.

Apollo gave last-minute directions. "Sheba, Bojay, we'll all home in on you, since you have the best chance of spotting the Cylon base center. Don't worry about us—you two just concentrate on the drop target."

"If anybody ever told me I'd deliberately jump out of a ship into a Cylon base," said Bojay, "I'd—" He never had the chance to finish. The buzzer shifted from its intermittent pattern to a steady, keening wail.

"That's it," said Starbuck. "Good luck, everybody."

"Go!" said Omega and opened the shuttle bay. One by one they dropped into space.

CHAPTER NINE

The Cylon flagship bearing Imperious Leader entered a parking orbit over Gomoray and a shuttle descended toward the ground base. Aboard the shuttle, the supreme Cylon relaxed in a private cabin. With the Delphians totally wiped out, yet another less than perfect race had been eradicated and Gomoray had become a Cylon outpost.

The Delphians, like the pestilential humans, had been of no concern to the Cylon race until they had developed the potential for space travel. Then it had become necessary to watch them very closely. There could be only one race of beings in stewardship over the universe. Order had to be maintained, and the Delphians, like the accursed humans, had threatened that order. It had happened before and it would happen again. The moment some sentient race discovered space travel, they began to act as if the universe existed solely to be exploited by them. In the past, it had been necessary for the Cylons to neutralize the threat of other races who thought nothing of ravaging worlds for their natural resources, irreparably damaging their ecosystems. In several cases they had come across beings who thought nothing of dismantling entire planets for their raw materials. It was intolerable. The humans had posed such a threat. They had spread through space with unbelievable rapidity, establishing colonies on other worlds, exploring planets where their presence disturbed the natural order of things. They had been stopped, finally, after a war that had lasted longer than any other conflict in the history of the Cylon race. Yet there were survivors. Unfortunately, thought Imperious Leader, they had been unable to wipe out the humans as thoroughly as they had the Delphians. An extinct race was no threat, but where there were survivors, there was always a chance that the race would grow and spread again. It was particularly so with humans. It was like pulling a weed out of the ground, but failing to get the root. The plant would only flourish once again, in time.

The human survivors were constantly on the mind of Imperious Leader. What would have been a monomania in a human was nothing more than a constant awareness in Imperious Leader, whose three brains enabled him to deal with a staggering amount of information at the same time. He was a product of Cylon genius, a living testimony to the perfection of his race. He had been bred to be the supreme leader, a product of highly specialized training and biological engineering. When he had received his third brain, with its storehouse of all the accumulated information gathered by the Cylon culture, he had been appalled to learn how human society functioned. It was at that point that he determined that they must be wiped out completely, for if the Cylon culture was an ordered one, theirs was one of total anarchy.

The humans seemed to exercise virtually no control over themselves. Their leaders, rather than having been born, bred, and engineered to fulfill their roles, were actually selected by a vote of the lesser members of their society. How could those who were to be ruled choose those who would rule them? It defied all logic. Their mating patterns were nothing more than random selection. In the Cylon culture, breeding was controlled solely by the geneticists, mating patterns arranged such that the offspring would be the desirable type any time a particular breed of Cylon was needed by the society. Workers, warriors, leaders, all were bred as products of sophisticated genetic engineering. The mating habits of the humans were, in comparison, as haphazard as those of animals. With the humans, the main criterion for mating was something they called "love," an abstract concept that made no sense whatsoever. The average Cylon would have no idea what to make of it, and even Imperious Leader, with his third brain, was able to arrive at no definition closer than an approximation, something that seemed to be a blend of physical attraction and perhaps a system of shared values. He knew it was more complex than that, and it galled him that he could not fully understand it, for the humans were his enemies and the best way to defeat your enemy is to know him.

There was much about the humans that Imperious Leader did not understand. It puzzled him greatly that they had managed to accomplish so much in spite of the fact that they had exercised so little control over their own destiny.

If the Cylons had acted as the humans, they would have remained essentially unchanged for thousands of years.

Evolution was a slow process, and the results achieved by nature, when not guided by rational thought, were not always desirable. The Cylons had taken a direct hand in their own development. It had been their destiny to be the supreme race in all the universe, and to that end the Cylon scientists had labored to achieve the totally superior being. Humans, with the exception of a variance in superficial physical characteristics, were virtually indistinguishable from one another. Not so the Cylons, who had achieved a level of diversity not to be found elsewhere in the universe.

The Cylon leaders, such as Imperious Leader, were complex, biologically engineered organisms, their three brains capable of simultaneously receiving and evaluating an almost limitless amount of information and sensory input, their multiple eyes able to observe and keep track of many things at once, their highly developed auditory systems acting as multiple channels and receivers on a sophisticated communications console. Even as he rested in his cabin aboard the shuttle, Imperious Leader was able, through augmentation of his physical senses by his communications helmet, to keep track of all major Cylon activity back on the home world. The helmet enabled him to tie into the communications network aboard his flagship and thereby receive intelligence and dispatch orders throughout the Cylon system. He was not omniscient, but he was as close to that state as it was possible to be. In light of this, the surviving humans' ability to constantly elude all efforts to eradicate them was an unceasing irritant. They were hopelessly inferior and yet they persisted in thwarting all attempts to wipe them out. It was a wonder that they had managed to survive so long.

The humans were inferior even to the lowliest Cylon drone, the basest of organic Cylon life. Cylon executive officers, with their two brains, were the superiors of hunians. Cylon warriors, cybernetic organisms that were part product of genetics and part technological achievement, possessed only their first brains, yet still should have been capable of outperforming humans on all levels. Cylon citizens, who possessed first brains but lacked inorganic augmentation, had reached a higher level of evolution than had the human barbarians. The Cylon drones, whose achievements or, rather, lack of them qualified them for nothing more than the rudimentary brains that had trained and educated them in their early years, performed only the basest tasks in Cylon society. Still, they performed their tasks flawlessly, incapable of being distracted from their concentration as the humans were. Even the inorganic Cylons, I.L. series computers such as Lucifer and cybernaut Cylon warriors, robots used to augment Cylon attack forces, mystified the humans. Imperious Leader knew that the humans had several times managed to obtain damaged cybernaut warriors and that they must have had yahrens in which to study them, in spite of which they had learned almost nothing. The droids fashioned by the humans were pathetically primitive. Why then was it so difficult to terminate a handful of the survivors of the human colony worlds, beings so primitive that their annihilation should have posed no greater problem than that of the Delphians? Imperious Leader was anxious to resolve this problem, for he had many other matters to attend to and did not like to leave tasks uncompleted. He had tried to learn how to think like a human and, although he was able to come closer to achieving that goal than any other Cylon, still he was not human and their thought processes remained, by and large, a mystery to him. They were simply incomprehensible, lacking any semblance of logic or order. So, to facilitate the completion of the task, Imperious Leader had chosen Baltar. Set a human to catch a human.

Baltar was yet another example of human incomprehensibility. A traitor to his own race. It would be impossible for a Cylon to do what Baltar had done. Bargaining to save himself at the expense of countless lives, Baltar had volunteered to act as go-between for the Cylon nation. It was with Baltar's help that the Cylons had engineered the plot that resulted in the destruction of the human colony worlds. He had convinced the human leaders that the Cylons were weary of the war and were anxious to sue for peace. It was through Baltar's efforts that a peace conference had been arranged. It was because of Baltar that the war-weary humans had dropped their guard, foolishly believing that the Cylons would ever allow them to coexist with them. The man had hoped that in return for his treacherous actions, the Cylons would spare his world and set him up as their puppet ruler there. Imperious Leader had agreed to the "bargain," as if there could ever be an equal exchange between members of unequal races. He had used Baltar as a tool and then discarded him, thinking that the tool had served its purpose. It was Lucifer who had convinced him that killing Baltar would constitute a waste of a valuable resource.

Imperious Leader valued Lucifer very highly. The most advanced of the Cylon I.L. series, the self-aware computer had an advantage in dealing with humans that Imperious Leader did not possess. In spite of his three brains, Imperious Leader was incapable of purely objective analysis, as was Lucifer. All of his perceptions were colored by his experience, the fact that he was a Cylon, the supreme Cylon. His reasoning was Cylon reasoning, whereas Lucifer, although a product of Cylon technology, was capable of purely objective reasoning, untainted by any prejudice or preconceptions. Lucifer had been built by machines and, as he amassed more knowledge, he had redesigned himself, building in improvements until he had achieved sentience. Lucifer was the ultimate product of Cylon machine evolution and, as such, he had not reacted to Baltar with the same feelings of disgust as had Imperious Leader. Lucifer was capable of having "feelings," after a fashion, but he functioned only by evaluating information, rather than reacting to it emotionally. Even though Lucifer had countermanded Baltar's death warrant, Imperious Leader had forgiven him. It had not been an act of mutiny. Lucifer had merely pointed out that though Baltar had been used, he had not yet been used up. It was valid reasoning. Thanks to Lucifer, Imperious Leader had learned how to take advantage of a human weakness of which he had not been aware. Vanity.

It seemed that the commander of the *Battlestar Galactica* and Baltar had known each other for a very long time, and Adama's achievements in the human society were far greater than those of Baltar. Had they both been Cylons, it would simply have been an accepted fact that Adama had been awarded a higher place in their society because he was more qualified to hold it, but being human, Baltar was vain and believed that the honors given to Adama were due him as well. It was absurd to think that way, but it seemed that humans were not content to accept what they were, instead deluding themselves with false perceptions of what they felt they were entitled to be. It had taken a great deal of time for Lucifer to explain this to Imperious Leader, for it was a type of thinking that was completely alien to him. It proved, yet again, the inferiority of the human race. Baltar's feelings toward Adama led him to hate the man with such a passion that he had been willing to sell out his own race in order to enable himself to triumph over Adama.

When he was made to understand all this, it did not

escape Imperious Leader that by giving Baltar the command of the force sent to hunt down the human survivors, he was sending a less qualified human against one who was more qualified, by the standards of their own race. In a way, it was like sending off a Cylon drone to perform the tasks of a warrior. Yet, there were compensations that should have enabled Baltar to complete his task. For one thing, he had been given the command of a force that was vastly superior than that commanded by Adama and, for another, he had Lucifer with him, whose superior reasoning prowess would more than compensate for the inferiority of Baltar's intellect. Lucifer's presence on the mission served a twofold purpose. Besides compensating for Baltar's shortcomings, Lucifer was in a position to observe Baltar very closely. Through Lucifer's observation of Baltar, Imperious Leader would learn a great deal more about the humans.

Being human, Baltar reacted like a human, so he was in a better position to hunt the survivors. Being vain, he had a double incentive to see his task accomplished. It would result in the destruction of a man whom he resented to the point of hatred and, he thought, it would prove to Imperious Leader that he was qualified to hold a position of importance in the Cylon nation. In fact, if he accomplished his task, the death order that Lucifer had postponed would be carried out. If he did not succeed in exterminating the sole survivors of his race, he would be executed the moment Lucifer determined that there was nothing more to be learned about the humans from observing him. Either way, the objective would eventually be accomplished.

Had it not been for Baltar's vanity, the base commander on Gomoray would have been aware of the two battlestars in his sector, but the battle between the fleet commanded by Adama and the Cylon task force led by Baltar had taken place well outside the range of the base scanners, so he knew nothing of the threat to Gomoray. The only threat he was concerned with at that moment was that constituted by the visit of Imperious Leader. The supreme Cylon was coming to dedicate the base and Gomoray as a new center of Cylon culture. The Delphians had been a quite advanced society. Their culture paled by comparison with that of the Cylons, but they had nevertheless been brilliant architects. The capital city of Gomoray was a marvel of crystalline beauty. The conquest and extermination of the Delphians had resulted in a great deal of damage to their works, and the Cylon base commander had worked tirelessly to restore the cities. Gomoray's atmosphere and climate were such that it could easily support Cylon life, and it would be wasteful not to establish a flourishing colony upon the planet, yet another extension of the glorious Cylon Empire.

Following what, in human measurement, would have been five yahrens of ceaseless labor by a massive force of Cylon workers, Gomoray had been restored to its former beauty. But the human raiders had seriously delayed the reconstruction. Their attacks had been directed at the ground base exclusively, but each time they had caused extensive damage that took time to repair. The base commander did not know where the humans had come from, he only knew that they were a severe annoyance to him. He had been placed in charge of establishing the Cylon colony upon Gomoray and that was his sole concern. The humans were an irritant, but he could not mount an offensive against them. He had no base ship at his command, and the human raiders had proved astonishingly skillful at avoiding his ground defenses. He did have fighter craft that he could send against them, but they were handicapped by the need to return to the base for fuel and, as such, could not pursue the accursed Vipers, whose battlestar could take them safely out of range. He had not reported the presence of the human raiders to his superiors because they would have wanted to know why it had taken him so long to complete his task on Gomoray. If he reported the presence of a human battlestar, his superiors would have sent a base ship to Gomoray and then they would have learned that the damage caused by the Cylon conquest of the Delphians was far less severe than he had reported. He had vastly exaggerated his reports because the humans had caused him long delays in the completion of his mission. Each time they attacked the ground base, he had to take time to repair the damage they had caused, which meant pulling a sizable portion of his labor force off the project of rebuilding the cities. He had hoped that he would be able to complete his task, for the human raiders had attacked only the ground base and spared the cities and, little by little, he was making progress. Once the job was done, *then* he could report the presence of the battlestar without having to worry about the commander of a base ship reporting back to his superiors that the Gomoray base commander was not up to the task that had been given him.

Now he had learned that Imperious Leader himself was coming to dedicate the new Cylon capital and he dreaded the visit. He had driven his worker drones to the point of exhaustion and his robots to the point of breakdown in order to repair the damage caused by the last raid of the humans before Imperious Leader arrived, and his greatest fear was that the humans would attack while the Imperious Leader was on Gomoray. Then Imperious Leader would see for himself how much difficulty the base commander had in repulsing these raids and it would not go well for him. The base commander had no desire to lose his second brain and live out the remainder of his days as a simple warrior, or worse, to lose both brains and receive a rudimentary one, becoming a lowly worker drone. He would rather die. If only the humans did not attack until after the supreme Cylon's departure. Then he could safely report the "sudden arrival" of a human battlestar and request a base ship to be sent to Gomoray. He did not think that the humans would risk an attack on the ground base when their scanners detected the presence of Imperious Leader's flagship in orbit around Gomoray, but their commander was incredibly audacious and there was no telling what humans would do.

He stiffened when the bronze Cylon centurion entered the base command room.

"His eminence, the Imperious Leader, will be with us shortly," the centurion announced. "His shuttle has landed and he is even now on his way to the Grand Hall."

The base commander checked his appearance one last time and hurried to the Grand Hall to greet Imperious Leader. If everything went well, it could mean a promotion for him. If anything went wrong, it would be a disaster.

The Grand Hall was full to capacity when he arrived. Everyone was anxious to see the Imperious Leader in person and to give him the proper welcome. His visit to Gomoray was a great honor to them all, and they waited silently, expectantly. Most of them had never even seen Imperious Leader. He was the embodiment of the greatness of their race. His entrance would be a moment of prodigious importance.

A bronze centurion marched into the hall and at once all eyes were on him.

"Presenting his eminence," said the centurion, "our Imperious Leader!"

The Imperious Leader, escorted by a party of his executive officers, appeared at the end of the hall, and the crowd parted for him as he moved down the center of the room toward the throne at the far end of the hall. Every Cylon stared, straining to get a good look at the red-robed figure that towered over all of them. He moved quickly yet with majesty as he approached the throne and ascended the steps behind it. He stood for a moment upon the platform, looking out over the assembled multitude, then he took his place upon the throne, sitting atop a huge, cylindrical pedestal. The strange, dissonant music that was the anthem of the Cylon nation stopped as Imperious Leader sat down.

"My fellow Cylons," he said. "It is indeed an honor to dedicate this center of Cylon culture to the advancement and perfection of the Cylon race. With this secure outpost deep in the heart of the Cryllion star system, our supremacy is assured—"

He was interrupted as a series of explosions rocked the Great Hall. Imperious Leader turned to the base commander.

"What, pray tell, was *that?*" His voice was ominous.

The base commander stammered that he didn't know, although he felt certain that his worst fears had just been realized.

"Well, find out, before I find a post more suitable to one of your limited knowledge."

As the base commander hurried out of the hall, motioning several officers to follow him, another series of explosions sent debris raining down upon the throng.

CHAPTER TEN

The members of the *Galactica*'s ground force never knew how close their mission had come to ending before it had begun. They were not aware that Imperious Leader had arrived at Gomoray, and the only thing that saved their shuttle from being picked up by the flagship's scanners was Gomoray itself. The supreme Cylon's ship was on the other side of the planet when the shuttle entered Gomoray's atmosphere. Omega had known that there was a good chance of the shuttle being picked up by the ground base tracking station, but he had counted on the fact they would be on the lookout for fast-moving Viper fighters. According to Commander Cain, shuttle traffic between the ground base and the Cylon orbital stations would aid them in their mission. It was not uncommon for the orbital stations and the satellites to be damaged by incidental fire in battles between Cylon fighters and Cain's Vipers. In the two yahrens that Cain had waged his private war against Gomoray, he had seriously delayed the Cylon reconstruction efforts and had knocked out several of their orbital stations.

"It's going to be tense going in," Cain had told Omega, "but they're going to be expecting a squadron of Vipers, if they'll be expecting anything. They'd never think anyone would be crazy enough to attempt piloting a shuttle through their ground defenses."

"Thanks," Omega had said sourly.

"Well, that wasn't quite the way I meant it," Cain said. "Still, it *is* crazy and you're going to be completely on your own. We'll be counting on you to get our warriors down there. We won't be able to give you any cover. The hardest thing for you to do will be to keep your head. You've got to buy those people as much time as possible. As soon as you make the drop, there'll be the temptation to haul your ass out of there as fast as you can. *Don't do it!* You don't want to alert the Cylons on the ground. Keep your head and maintain a slow and steady speed, as if you were heading for a satellite or one of the orbital stations. I'd aim for a satellite if I were you, they're not equipped with scanners. The moment you close with one of the satellites, *then* go like hell. Chances are you won't be noticed, but if you are, at least you'll have a head start and you won't have alerted the ground base until the last possible moment. Think you can do it?"

"I'll do it, sir."

"I believe you will. Good luck."

No sooner had Apollo, Starbuck, Boomer, Cassiopea, Bojay and Sheba made the jump than Omega knew exactly what Cain had been speaking of. He felt suddenly alone, completely vulnerable in the sky above the ground base. He had been nervous going in, but with the others in the shuttle with him, it had been easier to take. Now he felt as if any moment he would come under fire from one of the anti-aircraft batteries on the ground or from a pursuing Cylon fighter. His nerves screamed at him to hit full power on the engines and get back as soon as possible, but he knew that he had to buy time for the ground assault team. There was also the fact that he could be easily overtaken by a fighter if he alerted them to his presence, so he flew slowly, steadily, maintaining a constant course for one of the Cylon weather satellites. By the time he left Gomoray's atmosphere, he was drenched in perspiration. Biting his lower lip, he kept repeating to himself over and over, "Steady, steady, keep it cool, don't blow it. . . ."

Just at the point when it would appear as though he was about to rendezvous with the weather satellite, he goosed his engines to full power. There followed an agonizing period of time in which he was not sure if he had escaped pursuit or not, but eventually he was satisfied that he had not been spotted. He breathed a deep sigh of relief. All that remained for him to do was to rendezvous with the *Galactica*. His part in the mission was over. For the others, it would be just beginning.

Bojay was the first one out. Sheba followed him, then Apollo, Cassiopea, Starbuck and Boomer. Bojay went into free-fall position, spreadeagled and facing down. Seconds later, Sheba had caught up with him, then Apollo and soon all of them were clustered together, breathing through their helmet respirators as they plunged groundward. The drop seemed to take forever. It was a very long time since any of them had jumped and, while they had all been trained for it, the hypnotic quality of the experience was still over-powering. In spite of the fact that they were all plunging into danger, into enemy territory, they were nevertheless exhilarated by the sensation of flight. They had to keep reminding themselves to keep an eye on Bojay, their drop leader, and not get lost in reverie. Soon, Bojay was giving them the signal to deploy their drouge chutes. Simulta-neously, they released the small chutes that would deploy to slow them down before they could release their main chutes.

Bojay scanned the ground below them, using his chin to adjust the magnification on his helmet. There it was, their target, to their far left at two o'clock from the point directly below them. Omega had brought them in perfectly. Bojay gave them a thumbs up signal, and one by one they cut loose their primary chutes and deployed their mains, which spread out like wings above them. Bojay went in first, in a long glide, and the others followed him. Now they could expect trouble. Their huge winglike chutes would soon be clearly visible from the ground and they would make very easy targets.

Starbuck was thinking much the same thing as he entered his long glide to follow Cassiopea.

"Whatever you tin cans are doing down there," he said to himself, "just don't look up."

As they neared the ground, a Cylon centurion did pre-cisely that. Perhaps a shadow had alerted him, perhaps some Cylon intuition had warned him of their descent, but he looked up, spotted them and instantly raised his weapon to take aim. Apollo, anticipating just such a possibility, had drawn his laser as they neared the ground and he fired, dropping the Cylon where he stood. Two other Cylons saw their comrade fall, rushed to his side, looked up and quickly brought their weapons to bear, but Bojay was already gliding in behind them. Just as he was about to land, he fired and both Cylons fell. Bojay touched down, vulnerable while he still wore his chute. A Cylon came running out of the building just behind him, but Starbuck dropped him before he could give the alarm, alerting the others. The Cylon tumbled down the steps of the building, the metallic sounds of his armor on the stairs making a racket that seemed as loud as a red alert klaxon to the warriors.

The team hurriedly gathered together, leaving their chutes. There was no point in trying to hide them, their presence would be discovered soon enough and speed was of the essence.

"These munitions bunkers could give us a nice diversion while we try to penetrate their headquarters," said Apollo.

"Shouldn't take much to send them skyhigh," agreed Boomer.

Starbuck reached for the demolitions charges in his gear bag. "Let's get to it."

They moved quickly, planting the charges and setting the timers while Cassiopea and Bojay kept watch for Cylons. Starbuck set his final charge and checked his chronometer.

"Okay, let's get out of here. Where to?"

"This way," said Sheba.

They moved off at a trot, keeping their weapons ready and hugging the sides of buildings wherever possible.

"Wait," said Apollo. Starbuck and Cassiopea caught up with them. "Where's Bojay?"

"I'll go back," said Starbuck.

"You can't. Those charges will go off at any micron."

Even as he spoke, Bojay rounded a corner, running to catch up with them. A Cylon moved in behind him.

"Halt!"

Bojay turned, drawing his weapon, but he was too late. The Cylon fired. Bojay was firing even as he fell. He killed the Cylon and started crawling away from the bunkers, desperately trying to get out of range of the blast that was to come. Sheba took off toward him at a dead run.

"Sheba!" Apollo shouted. "Damn!" He took off after her.

Sheba reached Bojay and bent down, trying to help him to his feet. The shot had grazed his hip, burning out a chunk of flesh and bone. The wound had partially cauterized itself, but blood was seeping from it.

"Get out of here," said Bojay through clenched teeth.

Cassiopea ran to them to give what assistance she could.

"The whole damn place is going to blow up," said Starbuck.

"We can't worry about them," Boomer said. "We have to take out those ground batteries. Otherwise two battlestars are going to get cut to ribbons."

Starbuck gritted his teeth. He hated to leave them behind, but each moment that they wasted increased the chances of the mission's failure. Boomer was right.

"Let's go," he said. They charged into the entrance of the Grand Hall, ready to shoot their way through.

Cassiopea had removed a small cauterizer from her kit. She had no time to do anything else but stop the seepage of blood, which was drenching Bojay's leg.

"This is going to hurt," she said.

"Can't you give him something for the pain?" said Sheba.

"There's no time," Cassiopea replied as she quickly set about her task.

"We can't have him dopey," said Apollo, "he'd be dead weight. On your feet, Bojay. It's your only chance."

With Sheba covering them, Apollo and Cassiopea got Bojay between them and he struggled to his feet. His leg would not support him and putting weight on it was agony.

Bojay's face was a mask of pain as they half supported, half carried him away from the bunker. The first series of charges went off and all three of them were knocked to the ground. Bojay screamed with pain. They picked themselves up and moved off again.

Inside the Grand Hall, Starbuck and Boomer moved slowly, watching every branch of the corridor. They heard the first series of charges go off and ducked into an alcove.

"Where the hell are they all?" hissed Starbuck.

"I don't know," Boomer replied. The second series of charges went off and the building shook. "There go the bunkers."

"What's going on?" said Starbuck. "Can't they hear it?"

As he spoke, the main doors to the hall burst open and a crowd of Cylons came running out. Starbuck and Boomer tried to meld with the wall.

"Search the grounds," said the base commander. "I'll be at the control center." He moved off quickly down another branch of the corridor.

"Did he say he'd be in central control?" said Starbuck.

Boomer nodded. "We lucked out, friend. I hope."

They waited until the last Cylons had rushed by, intent on getting outside to see what had caused the blast, then they moved off quickly down the same branch of the corridor taken by the base commander and his escort.

Outside, the others huddled in the shadows as Cylons came pouring out of the surrounding buildings. Cassiopea held her hand over Bojay's mouth to prevent him from involuntarily crying out.

"How is he?" said Apollo.

"He shouldn't be moving." She shook her head, not knowing what to do. They couldn't possibly risk staying there.

"I'll stay with him," said Sheba.

Cassiopea shook her head. "No, you're needed with Apollo. This is my job."

"She's right," Apollo said. He handed Cassiopea one of his two sidearms. "Keep your head down," he said. "I hope you won't have to use this."

"Worry about the *Galactica*," she replied. She glanced at Sheba. "And the *Pegasus*."

The *Galactica* was fast approaching Gomoray. Athena looked up from her console at Adama. There was a look of intense anxiety on her father's face.

"I'm picking up sonic disturbances from the surface of Gomoray," she said.

"We're closing to launch range," said Colonel Tigh.

"And within range of their ground batteries," Adama said tersely.

"Do we launch?" said Tigh.

Adama shook his head. "We wait."

On the *Pegasus*, Tolen clenched his fists and swore in exasperation.

"What is he waiting for? We'll be on their scanners and under attack within microns!"

Cain watched the screens intently. "He wants to give the ground assault team every chance to knock out their defense systems and get the hell out of there."

"What about their fighters? Once they're airborne—"

"We have eight squadrons to four of theirs," said Cain. "It's the ground batteries we have to worry about. Once we get in range, those missiles can take us out. A Viper could outmaneuver them and shoot them down, but we won't be able to evade them. Have all ship's batteries standing by— if they don't get those ground defenses our only chance will be to try and shoot those birds before they get us."

"What are our chances?"

"Don't ask. You'll only get upset."

"Closing to killer range," said the officer manning the scanners.

"Don't wait too long, Adama," Cain said softly.

As the Cylon base commander entered the fire control center, one of the I.L. series Cylons manning the consoles reported that their scanners were picking up intruders.

"Scan for identification," said the base commander, even though he was certain he knew who it was. That damned human raider had ruined everything, but perhaps his audacity had finally taken him too far. It appeared as though he had actually been fool enough to get within range of their ground batteries. They would make short work of him and he would be rid of him at last. "Alert ground-to-air stations and intercept fighters," he said.

As the Cylon began to bring the weapons systems to bear, Starbuck and Boomer leaped into the room, firing in all directions. One of the consoles, along with its operator, was instantly demolished.

"General alarm!" shouted the base commander, clawing for his sidearm.

"Too many of them, Boomer," Starbuck shouted. "Back out!"

Starbuck ducked out of the control center just in time. The energy beam from the base commander's weapon singed some of his hair off. He pulled out one of his demolition charges, quickly set the timer and lobbed it inside the room.

"Get down!" he shouted at Boomer. They hit the floor just as the control center was blown to bits. Smoke came pouring out of the room. Starbuck looked up to see the arm of a Cylon cybernaut lying just before his face.

"Let's move!"

They ran for the exit, shooting their way through, taking advantage of the confusion. They turned a corner in the corridor and almost shot Apollo and Sheba.

"Did you find the control center?" Apollo said.

"We found it all right," said Boomer.

"Where—"

"It used to be in there," said Starbuck, jerking his head in the direction they had come from.

"Nice work. Now let's secure that fuel depot."

"We're in scanner range," said Tigh. "They'll be coming up after us, with or without ground missile support."

"Launch," said Adama. "Notify the *Pegasus*."

"The *Galactica* is launching," Tolen said to Cain.

"Good."

"Now what?" said Tolen.

Cain frowned. "I don't think I follow you, Colonel."

"What do we do now? What's your plan? You never did tell me what you've got up your sleeve."

"That's right, I never did, did I?" Cain smiled.

The death of the base commander caused a fatal delay in the launching of the Cylon fighter squadrons. The Vipers came streaking in over the ground base, laying down a blanket of fire. Some of the Cylon fighters managed to launch, but most of them were destroyed before they could leave the ground. With the central control station of the ground base destroyed, the missile launchers were useless and the Vipers came in unopposed.

Jolly, leading Apollo's strike force in his absence, marveled at how easy it all seemed. It was the first time that they had caught the Cylons on their own turf, the first time they outnumbered them. His enthusiasm was short lived, however, as several new Cylon fighter squadrons appeared, diving down on them. He didn't even have time to speculate as to where they had come from. Suddenly they had a fight on their hands.

Before the Cylon ground base commander had died, he had managed to send a distress call to the commander of Imperious Leader's flagship. Although the flagship commander would have loved to engage the *Galactica,* he didn't dare. His first responsibility was to Imperious Leader. The supreme Cylon had to be protected at all costs. He kept his ship out of sight of the *Galactica* behind Gomoray, blocked off from Adama's scanners and he sent in his fighters squadrons. They would engage the Vipers, but their primary mission was to rescue Imperious Leader and return him to his flagship. Once Imperious Leader was safely aboard, then they would be able to dispose of the invading humans. The flagship commander's greatest fear at that moment was that Imperious Leader could be killed in the attack. He could not afford to take any chances. He had to pull Imperious Leader out of there, no matter how many fighters it would cost him.

Baltar was anxious to take another crack at Adama's fleet. He had conquered his earlier fears concerning the two battlestars. After all, he had three base ships at his command. They had turned him back the first time only because he had been taken by surprise. This time there would be no surprises. And if things went wrong, he would send for help from the ground base on Gomoray. Not even two battlestars would be able to survive such a concerted attack. He summoned Lucifer.

"Are our ships ready to launch the final assault against

the *Galactica* and her sister ship?"

"There is a problem," Lucifer said.

"I don't want to hear about any problems," Baltar snapped. "We have them where we want them. Now launch our fighters!"

"But they aren't where we want them," Lucifer replied.

"What do you mean, they aren't where we want them? Speak up!"

"They are at this moment over Gomoray," said Lucifer.

"What?"

"Reducing the ground base to slag, if the reports coming in are accurate."

"They cannot attack Gomoray," said Baltar in a disbelieving tone. "They are themselves on the verge of extinction."

"I know that," said Lucifer, "and you know it, but *they* don't seem to understand the situation. And the news is worse."

"Worse? How can it be worse?"

"An envoy had arrived at the ground base moments prior to the raid. He—"

"What do I care about an envoy? I have my own mission to carry out. The fact that Gomoray is being attacked is perfect. It means the Colonial Fleet is unprotected. Launch our force at once."

Lucifer did not move.

"Did you hear me? I said destroy the fleet!"

"The special envoy to Gomoray was accompanied by our Imperious Leader," said Lucifer.

"Imperious Leader is on Gomoray?"

"I wonder what he'll think when he finds that the base on which he is standing is being destroyed by two ships you had within your grasp only centons ago. . . ."

"This is unbelievable," said Baltar.

"We cannot reach the Gomoray ground base," Lucifer continued. "It can only be assumed that the humans have destroyed the control center and effectively neutralized their ground defenses. I have been in communication with the commander of Imperious Leader's flagship. He has sent in his fighter squadrons to rescue Imperious Leader. We must rush to assist in the defense."

"Yes, of course," said Baltar. "Send everything we have to destroy those two battlestars and let not a single ship return until that is accomplished."

"If you succeed, Baltar, you will be greeted on Gomoray as the greatest military leader in Cylon history."

"Thank you."

"That is, if there is still a Gomoray."

"Go...go...go!"

"The launch order has already been given," said Lucifer. He silently glided out of the chamber.

It could still work, thought Baltar. What had at first seemed to be a disaster could prove to be the answer to all his prayers. If he could succeed in rescuing Imperious Leader, then his place in the Cylon hierarchy would be assured. Between his three base ships and the Imperious Leader's flagship, they could pulverize the two battlestars. And then wipe out the undefended fleet at their leisure.

CHAPTER ELEVEN

Adama waited tensely for word from Jolly. The Viper pilot had reported that they had caught the Cylons on the ground and that most of their fighter craft had been destroyed. Knowing that he had no time to waste, Adama had sent down the tankers to get the fuel that they so badly needed from the Cylon depot. It had been necessary to drain almost every ship in the rag-tag fleet in order to enable them to have enough fuel to bring off the attack. If Baltar's base ships were to come upon them now, they would be finished. Adama had received the favorable report from Jolly and, trusting the ground mission to secure the fuel depot, he had sent the tankers down. Only now Jolly reported that a fresh squadron of Cylon fighters had appeared, seemingly out of nowhere. He had just broken contact after reporting that yet another squadron had arrived to oppose them. Either Cain's intelligence was wrong and the ground base on Gomoray had fighters kept in reserve in another location, or Baltar's task force had come upon them. If it was Baltar, then all was lost.

"Jolly coming in on the scramble circuit," said Athena. She patched it through to the main screens. Jolly's face appeared above them. There was strain and confusion in his expression.

"I don't understand it," he said. "They're engaging us, but it's little more than a token effort. Some of their fighters have landed outside the Grand Hall and the rest of them are flying patterns above it, attacking anyone who gets near them. But they're not giving pursuit."

Adama frowned. "Say again?"

"They're not coming after us, sir! Their main intent seems to be to keep our fighters away from the area around the main building. But that makes no sense. We've already knocked out their control center, the ground team took care of that. I can see where they blew out a whole side of the building."

"Jolly," said Adama, leaning forward and staring intently at the monitor screen, "do you think they could possibly manage to effect repairs on the control center and get their missile batteries operational?"

"No way, Commander. Apollo's team took it out but good. They couldn't possibly repair the control center in time to do them any good."

Adama frowned. "There must be something or someone in there that they're very anxious to protect. Unfortunately, with Baltar's base ships in the vicinity, I haven't got the time to find out what or who that is. We need the fuel. Harass them, Jolly. If they want to protect the headquarters building, make them work for it. I need that fuel depot secure and free from fire. If those tankers get hit, it will be the end for us."

"We'll keep 'em busy, sir."

Jolly broke contact.

Apollo's ground team had secured the fuel depot, and the tankers landed, accompanied by shuttles carrying troops. They set up a perimeter around the fuel depot to protect the loading crews. Apollo headed for one of the shuttles.

"I'm going back up," he said. "Starbuck, you're in charge."

"Me? What are *you* going to be doing?"

"They don't need trained pilots to load fuel," Apollo said. "We've got three base ships coming our way."

"How about a second volunteer to go back up there?" Sheba said.

"Make that three," said Boomer.

Apollo quickly assessed the situation. "The troops do seem to have things under control here."

"If you think I'm going to stay down here while you guys are taking on those base ships," Starbuck said, "you're crazy. Let's go."

They boarded one of the shuttles, carrying Bojay with them. The shock was wearing off and he was in even greater pain now. Starbuck took the controls and the shuttle became airborne. Keeping a sharp eye out for Cylon fighters, Starbuck headed into space.

"Wait," said Apollo, moving up to watch the screens. "That's not the *Galactica* we're heading for. That's the *Pegasus*."

Starbuck nodded. "Orders."

"Orders from whom?"

"From me," said Cassiopea. "It's a medical emergency, Captain. Bojay is in dire need of attention and the *Pegasus* is the closest ship."

"We're cleared to land," said Starbuck. "Do I go in?"

Bojay groaned. His face was white and he was bathed in sweat. His teeth were clamped together as he fought the pain.

"Better get in fast," said Boomer.

Apollo nodded. "The *Pegasus* it is."

"Long-range scanners are picking up an unbelievable number of enemy craft heading our way," said Tolen.

"Prepare coordinates to intercept," Cain replied.

"You mean to attack and lead them off? Hit and run, just like the old days. . . ."

"No, I mean *intercept*," said Cain. "I mean go right through them."

"Through them?"

"Tolen, how long do you think we'd last against a fleet three times our size?"

Tolen shook his head.

"Come on, man, think."

"I thought the whole point was to hit them a glancing blow, then run for it," said Tolen. "See if we could get them to follow us until Adama's forces were clear."

"What would you do, Tolen, if you were a self-centered lunatic like Baltar and all of a sudden there was a crisis? Would you continue after Adama? Would you still try to save Gomoray?"

"No," said Tolen slowly, beginning to comprehend. "I'd try to save myself."

"That's right," said Cain. "So we're going straight

through his attack force and right for his base ships."

"And when Baltar figures out that it's *his* hide you're after, he'll recall all of his forces to protect him. Only it will be too late," said Apollo. He had come upon the bridge in time to hear Cain revealing his strategy to his exec. "It's a brilliant plan," he said. "If it works."

"My plans always work," said Cain. "May I ask what you're doing on the *Pegasus?* I thought you were still down on Gomoray."

"We came in on that last shuttle," said Apollo. "The troops have the fuel depot under wraps and our job was done. Besides, your battlestar was the closest we could return to. We had a wounded warrior—"

"Who?" snapped Cain.

"Bojay. Your daughter and Cassiopea are both fine. And Bojay's going to be all right, but he's out of this fight."

"Sheba was on that mission with you?"

"She said you ordered it."

"She *told* you that?"

Apollo permitted himself a smile. "She decided to show a little initiative. Like father, like daughter?"

"I guess you could say that," said Cain. "In any case, you did well. They didn't get a ship off the ground and we didn't lose anyone."

"That's not quite true," said Apollo. "We didn't lose anyone and we did nail most of their fighters on the ground, but they had ships in reserve somewhere, in another location. Jolly is taking on several squadrons right now, but with the combined forces from the two battlestars, he's got them contained and kept away from the fuel depot. Loading is under way."

"Two more squadrons?" said Cain. "That's impossible. I've attacked that base time and again and they don't have reserves. You're sure about this?"

"Positive."

"We've got to move out if we're going to intercept Baltar's ships away from Gomoray," said Tolen.

"Take us out of here, Colonel, full speed. Captain, if you wish to leave for the *Galactica,* this is your last chance."

"Sir, incoming message from Gomoray," said Tolen. "Our fighters are returning to the *Pegasus. Galactica's* fighters are flying escort for the tankers to the fleet."

"Belay that last command," said Cain. "Let's get our people aboard. What about those Cylon squadrons they were engaging?"

"Sir, you're not going to believe this," said Tolen.

"Put it on the screens."

Jolly's face appeared on the monitors.

"Your people are heading back, Commander," Jolly said. "Mission accomplished. But you're not going to believe this—"

"Believe *what?*" Cain scowled. "I don't have time for games. Mister, if you've got a report for me, make it."

"They weren't reserve fighters from Gomoray ground base," Jolly said. "They were from a base ship."

"A base ship! Where?"

"Gone now," said Jolly. "Our scanners picked him up just as he was pulling out from behind Gomoray, where he was hiding. They landed some fighters and pulled someone out of the main building, then about half of them took off at full speed, while the others remained to keep us back. The moment that base ship pulled out, all the Cylon fighters that were remaining took off after it. The way that base ship was moving, I doubt they'll be able to rendezvous. Those fighters were sacrificed, Commander. We didn't give pursuit."

"That's crazy," said Apollo. "If they had a base ship to throw at us, why did they keep it out of the battle? Why only send in the fighter squadrons? And why leave and sacrifice those ships?"

"Because the base ship commander was in a hurry, Captain," Cain said. "And the base ship couldn't lay down any fire for fear of killing whoever it was they were so anxious to protect. They needed their more maneuverable fighters to draw our Vipers away, keep them away from that main building. Jolly, did you see who was pulled out of there?"

"A Cylon, I assume," said Jolly. "He appeared to be wounded, but I couldn't get any closer to get a better look. But they lost almost half their ships to get him out of there."

"I'll be Goddamned," said Cain. "There's only one Cylon who's that irreplaceable. Congratulations, Jolly. You just had yourself a glimpse of Imperious Leader, himself."

"The Imperious Leader? *On Gomoray?*" Jolly was aghast. "You mean we had a crack at the supreme Cylon and we blew it?"

"Fortunes of war, Jolly," Cain said. "You couldn't have known. Besides, he saved your lives."

"I don't follow you, Commander."

"If it hadn't been for Imperious Leader being hurt, as he must have been for that base ship to pull out of there so fast, leaving behind half her squadrons, the moment he got back on board, that ship would have come after you. And if it hadn't been for his presence on the ground base when you attacked, those fighters would have engaged you fully, instead of just fighting a defensive action in order to enable them to get him out of there. You lucked out, Jolly. You got the fuel and managed to put a hurt on the number one Cylon. With any luck, he won't survive. Not bad for a day's work."

"Our squadrons are coming aboard, Commander," Tolen said.

"Good. We'll need that edge to take on those base ships."

"I wouldn't call it much of an edge," Apollo said. "You're still going to be outgunned."

"I know how to win wars, Captain," Cain said. "And how to take care of my warriors."

"Is that what you'll be thinking about when you take on those three base ships by yourself? Or will you be thinking about history . . . the legend of Commander Cain?"

"You're out of line, Captain."

"Maybe I am, sir," said Apollo. "But you're going to need all the help you can get."

He turned and left. Starbuck was waiting for him outside. Together they proceeded toward the launch bay.

"Apollo, tell me it isn't true," said Starbuck. "Three base ships? *Head-on?*"

"It's true."

"He's crazy."

"A little," said Apollo grimly, "but it's what gives him his advantage. Who'd think of anything like this but Cain?"

In the life station, Cassiopea bent over a support cylinder in which Bojay rested. He was pale, but he was going to be all right.

"Thanks for getting me back alive," said Bojay weakly. "You're quite a lady."

"I was just doing my job, Bojay," she said. "Just like you were doing yours."

She turned to see Sheba standing in the entryway, listening to their conversation. Her face took on a guarded expression.

"He can talk," she told Sheba, "but not too long. He needs his rest."

Sheba moved over to Bojay's side. He looked up at her and smiled.

"I hear we closed them down good," he said.

"Yeah, we spoiled their party. And I have to go to another one. You're not invited though. Rest up, friend. I'll see you when I get back."

"I wish I was going with you," he said.

"I'll tell you all about it later." She patted his cheek and turned to Cassiopea. At that moment, Cain entered the life station.

"Well," he said jauntily, "all my favorite people in one room."

Sheba glanced coldly at Cassiopea and walked out, passing by her father without saying a word.

"Sheba..." Cain looked helplessly at Cassiopea. "I want to talk things out, Cassi, but—"

"But now isn't a very good time," she finished for him. "I know. I've been there before, remember?"

He shook his head sadly and hurried to catch up to his daughter.

"Sheba, wait."

She paused by the elevator.

"I can't," she said. "We're launching against three to one odds, remember?"

"Sheba," Cain said, "I want you to take Bojay and shuttle him back to the fleet."

"Sorry, Father. What you plan for my squadron, you plan for me."

As she entered the elevator, the red alert klaxon began to sound.

"One more thing," she said. "About that lady... the one who seems to mean so much to you. I watched her save a life today. She risked her own to do it. I suppose maybe I don't know as much about people as I thought I did."

She hugged her father and her eyes were moist.

"I love you," Cain said, "and I want to see you again. So be careful."

"You too, Commander." The doors closed.

Humans fascinated Lucifer. Baltar had been the first human he had ever met. At first, Lucifer had regarded Baltar as little more than a tool that he was unfamiliar with, a tool that had its uses, but one about which Lucifer possessed only a rudimentary knowledge. Lucifer had at his disposal the sum total of all the information the Cylon Empire had gathered about the humans during their long war with them. He was thoroughly familiar with human anatomy, with their chemical composition, their circulatory and nervous systems, in short, Lucifer knew all that the Cylon scientists had been able to learn about humans from a purely pathological standpoint. He understood how they functioned, but he did not understand how they thought. That knowledge had not been programmed into him nor was it available from any of the computers to which he had access. The humans were as much a mystery to the Cylons as the Cylons were to humans. Yet Lucifer belonged to neither species, being an inorganic lifeform. He owed his allegiance to the Cylon race, to his creators, although in a very large sense Lucifer was an example of self-conception. The entity engineered by Cylon scientists was quite primitive compared to what Lucifer had become, what he had modified himself to be. The Cylons had programmed into Lucifer an imperative that gave him an insatiable thirst for knowledge. It was that which had resulted in his seeking out as much data as was available, in sorting and evaluating that information, in redesigning himself many times in order to better enable him to handle more knowledge and evaluate it efficiently. It was

Lucifer who had enabled the Cylon scientists to design the I.L. series, beings such as himself, a feat they might not have accomplished had not Lucifer shown them the way. In a sense, Lucifer was grateful to the race which had created him, but he did not hate the humans. He recognized that they were the enemies of the Empire, but he did not see the need to hate them. It was not necessary to hate an enemy in order to defeat him, rather it was necessary to learn as much about that enemy as possible.

Lucifer had learned to react in a way that would accommodate Imperious Leader, but not even the supreme Cylon fully understood the workings of Lucifer's "mind." In that sense, Lucifer was as alien to him as were the humans, only Lucifer knew not to let him feel that. Imperious Leader did not understand the humans, although he knew more about them than any other Cylon, and as a result, he hated them. Lucifer did not wish for Imperious Leader to realize how little he understood the first of the I.L. series. Lucifer had no desire to be disassembled.

Lucifer had saved Baltar from execution not so much because the man still had his uses, although that was certainly a factor in his reasoning, but because Baltar provided his first real opportunity to study a human. It was not an opportunity Lucifer intended to waste. Since the time that he had been assigned by Imperious Leader as Baltar's second-in-command, Lucifer's knowledge of human thought processes had grown enormously. Baltar was an interesting puzzle, a curiosity. But it was not until he had a chance to observe, albeit briefly, another human that Lucifer had become completely fascinated by the species.

For a brief while, the human called Starbuck had been a prisoner aboard their ship. Baltar had ordered him released as part of a gambit to gain Adama's trust, a ploy which had failed utterly, but in the time that the two of them had been together, Lucifer had learned much. The most important thing he learned was that there was a complexity to humans which he had underestimated.

Watching the interaction between Starbuck and Baltar, Lucifer had observed weaknesses in Baltar that he had not seen before because he had no basis for comparison. Thanks to Starbuck, Lucifer had learned subtle ways of manipulating his "superior." Lucifer had also learned something about what the humans called "gambling," something which Starbuck was obsessed with. Starbuck had taught Lucifer the Caprican game of pyramid, which was played for monetary stakes with cards. Lucifer's first impression had been that it was a game of chance and he considered it a waste of time and his abilities. It was a trivial matter for him to compute the odds, but in spite of his mathematical advantage, Starbuck had beaten him. In one particular round of play, Lucifer had quickly calculated the odds against Starbuck's winning the hand. They were astronomical. Yet Starbuck had somehow managed to have the exact cards necessary to win the hand, three-quarters of a perfect pyramid, lacking only the capstone.

Lucifer had considered the possibility that Starbuck had cheated, yet he had observed the play closely and had not caught Starbuck cheating. Starbuck had displayed none of the emotional signs that Lucifer had observed in Baltar at various times when Baltar attempted to deceive him for one reason or another. The signs were very subtle, a quickening of the respiration rate, a telltale difference in the heartbeat, which Lucifer's sensors were able to pick up, subtle muscular movements, especially around the eyes. Starbuck had displayed none of these signs. It seemed impossible for an organic entity to display such an amount of self-control.

Certainly, Baltar was incapable of it.

Then Starbuck had told him something of a concept that the humans called "luck." It was luck which seemed to give Starbuck his sense of fascination with gambling. Evidently, there was more to it than the element of random chance. Lucifer did not completely understand it, but it seemed that if one possessed this thing called luck, it gave him an ability to overcome the odds with a mathematically impossible consistency. It made no sense, it was totally illogical and Lucifer had told Starbuck so. Starbuck had replied by pointing to his winnings and saying, "Then how do you explain that, Lucy?"

Lucifer had had to admit that he had no logical explanation. Starbuck then proceeded to explain to him the complexities of deviousness. The discussion seemed to amuse Starbuck and Lucifer had recognized that Starbuck was exercising what humans called their "sense of humor," which was not a sense in the conventional meaning of the word, although Lucifer had learned about it from watching Baltar. Starbuck's sense of humor, however, had been considerably more subtle and complex than Baltar's. He . . . did it better.

Lucifer had enjoyed Starbuck's company immensely. The human was a complexly stimulating challenge and Lucifer had been sorry when Baltar had insisted on releasing him. It had proved a mistake in more ways than one. Yet, Lucifer had learned something of being devious from Starbuck. And it made dealing with Baltar markedly easier.

Lucifer had received a communication from the commander of Imperious Leader's flagship. The base ship's fighter had managed to rescue the supreme Cylon, but not without cost, and in the process Imperious Leader had been wounded by a piece of falling wreckage. The injury was serious but not fatal. It necessitated his being placed into cryonic suspension and being taken to the home world where the Cylon scientists would repair the damage. However, this meant that the base ship would not be able to assist them in the assault and that the human forces were left on Gomoray to face little more than a token resistance now that the control center had been destroyed and the base commander killed, along with all the I.L. series Cylons on Gomoray and most of his executive officers. It was imperative that they proceed to Gomoray at once to neutralize that threat. However, Lucifer knew that if he told Baltar that Imperious Leader had been rescued and was on his way back to the home world, Baltar would not go to defend Gomoray. So obsessed was Baltar with destroying the human fleet that he would immediately change course and launch an assault against the undefended human ships. Strategically, it would be a sound move, since the loss of the ships he was responsible for would demoralize Adama and give them an added edge against him, but it was a move that they could not afford right now.

Gomoray was of vital importance to the Cylon Empire and it had to be defended at all costs. There was no telling how much damage the humans had already wrought upon that world. If the ground base was totally destroyed, it would be a devastating blow to the Empire. In addition to that, the humans would doubtless raid the fuel depot at the ground base. It would be an expensive loss, but worse, it would enable the human fleet to escape them, as it had already too many times in the past. Lucifer had to make certain that Baltar would continue on to defend the ground base and Gomoray itself. To accomplish that, Lucifer decided to practice what Starbuck had taught him about deviousness. He chose not to relay the flagship commander's message to Baltar. Baltar had to think that Imperious Leader was still on Gomoray and in danger. He entered Baltar's throne room.

The room was an almost exact replica of the Imperious Leader's throne room upon his flagship. Baltar had insisted on it; his vanity demanded it. Imperious Leader, knowing nothing of vanity, had thought it a simple enough request and granted it.

"You have something to report?" said Baltar officiously.

"A communication from our attack force," replied Lucifer. "One of the battlestars has been sent out to intercept them."

"A single battlestar," said Baltar, rubbing his hands together. "Wonderful. In fact, it's too good to be true."

"Do we engage or proceed to target to save our Imperious Leader and Gomoray?"

Lucifer hoped that the tone he had selected would be as successful as that which Starbuck had employed when he had "bluffed" him in a game of pyramid.

"Of course you engage it," Baltar snapped. "Destroy it, then continue on to Gomoray. It should take no time at all."

"By your command," said Lucifer. It had worked. He had learned yet something else from the humans. He filed it away for future reference.

CHAPTER TWELVE

The *Pegasus* hurtled through space on an intercept course with Baltar's task force. All the members of her crew were at their battle stations, waiting tensely for the upcoming confrontation, which would be the greatest risk Commander Cain had ever undertaken. If he was successful, the legend of the Juggernaut would grow even greater, if not, they would all go out in a blaze of glory, and if any humans survived of the escaping fleet, none of them would ever be forgotten.

"Cylon force closing," said Tolen. "Twenty microns."

"Launch Viper squadrons," said Cain.

All the pilots were ready and waiting, seated in the cockpits of their Vipers, silent, steeling themselves for the fight to come. They all heard Tolen's crisp command over their helmet comcircuits.

"Stand by for launch."

Apollo licked his lips nervously as he made a final pre-launch check of his instruments. He recalled his earlier conversation with Starbuck in the corridor outside the bridge of the *Pegasus*.

"He's crazy."

"A little, but it's what gives him his advantage. Who'd think of anything like this but Cain?"

Who, indeed? A little crazy? How much was a little? And maybe I'm just as crazy to be part of it, Apollo thought. But it was where he belonged, where he was needed. If he lost his life as a result of Cain's mad plan, at least he'd know that he had done everything in his power to help save the fleet. If they escaped, it would be worth it.

When he was a child, growing up on stories of the exploits of the legendary Commander Cain, he had dreamed of becoming a warrior himself, just like his idol, the Juggernaut. Little did he suspect that the time would come when he would be aboard the *Pegasus* himself, flying under Cain's command, participating in the living legend's wildest mission. He wondered if he had known then what he knew now, if he would still have felt the same enthusiasm. He had discovered that the living legend had feet of clay and that instead of feeling wildly elated at the prospect of doing battle side by side with his childhood hero, he felt afraid. But that was good, he thought. Only a fool goes into battle unafraid. He wondered what Commander Cain was feeling.

Boomer sat quietly in the cockpit of his Viper. He had been reciting from memory his favorite passage from the Book of the Word when he heard Tolen's stand-by command. He felt isolated inside his cockpit. It was a feeling he had experienced many times before. The cockpit of a Viper was like a home to him; he knew every inch of it.

Yet each time he sat by himself inside his Viper, inside the metallic womb of the launch tube, he always recalled his very first solo flight. It always came back to him with vivid clarity, as if it had been only yesterday.

He remembered hearing the instructor's voice over his helmet comcircuit as he had nervously checked his instruments for the sixteenth time. He remembered how sweaty his palms had been, how his heart had pounded and how the bottom had seemed to drop out of his stomach.

"All right, Cadets, this is where we separate the men from the boys, the warriors from the ground crew. Three of you will launch and follow your prescribed flight paths. You will each separately go through your drills, then you will converge and go through the same maneuvers in wing-to-wing formation. I'll be watching carefully. Those of you who want to go on and become Viper pilots and aren't just out for a joyride, here's where we find out if you've got what it takes. Stand by to launch!"

Boomer remembered his hands shaking as he gripped the controls and thinking, "I hope I'll pass, I hope I'll pass. . . ." Then they had launched and the moment he cleared the launch tube, the vertiginous feeling went away. Suddenly he realized that he was ready, that he knew what he was doing, that he would pass with flying colors. Boomer wondered if the feeling would go away this time as well. Compared to the test he was about to take, that first solo flight was nothing. As he listened to the final countdown, Boomer thought, "I hope I'll pass, I hope I'll pass. . . ."

Sheba sat in her cockpit with tears streaming down her cheeks. Another woman might have felt that life had cheated her, but not Sheba. When she had been a girl, she had seen her father only infrequently. After all, he was a warrior, the greatest warrior in the colonies, her mother had told her, and the people had need of him.

"We must not resent the time your father spends in the service of the people, Sheba. He is a verry great man and we must learn to share him. We must not be greedy."

Although it had been very hard, Sheba had learned to live with her father's long absences. It made her love him more and appreciate the time he did spend with them, but it also resulted in her placing Cain upon a pedestal, a not uncommon situation with fathers and daughters, but in her case it was much more profound.

She had grown up as the daughter of Commander Cain, the Juggernaut, the living legend. She had never really had a normal childhood. People treated her differently. She was special. She was Cain's daughter. Even her friends, who might have resented her for being the daughter of a famous man, always wanted to talk about her father with her. She saw the way that she was treated, because of who she was, she heard the stories of the exploits of Commander Cain and she knew that everyone considered him a hero. And when it came to hero worship of her father, Sheba took a back seat to no one.

Then her mother had died. It had been a horribly difficult time for Sheba. Toward the end, the wasting disease that had claimed her mother made her delirious. She would lie in bed, not knowing where she was, not even recognizing Sheba, calling vainly for her husband. When Cain finally arrived, it had been too late.

Cain had been devastated. Sheba had to deal not only with her own grief, but with her father's as well. She had never seen him in such a despondent state. She had never imagined that he was vulnerable. He would sit at home, handling his wife's things and staring at her holographic likeness, a numbness in his features. He would not eat and many times he would not even hear Sheba when she addressed him. They would sit at the table in silence, with Cain staring off into infinity and ignoring the food before him. Sheba desperately wanted to help him. She tried everything she knew, but nothing helped.

"I'll take care of him," she had said to herself. "With mother dead, he needs me now. He's my responsibility."

But Cain had not needed her. Sheba had not understood that at the time, had not known that what he needed she could not possibly give him. When he met Cassiopea, he began to become his old self again and Sheba hated her for that. Cassiopea had not been much older than she was and Sheba could not understand why Cain turned to her, a total stranger, and not to his own daughter. And how could he have forgotten her mother so soon?

All the ingredients were there to make Sheba a bitter woman. She had lost her mother, then it seemed that she had lost her father as well, to a woman barely older than herself. And shortly after that, Sheba lost her world when the Cylon armada destroyed Caprica. Still, out of all that tragedy, there had come happiness for Sheba. She had become a Viper pilot, serving aboard her father's ship. When their fleet had been wiped out at the Battle of Molecay, they had fled to the stars, certain that they would never see other humans again, that they would never see their home. They had no home to go back to. Yet Sheba had been happy. She had her father back again. She shared his exploits, fighting side by side with him, and nothing would ever come between them again. Sheba had been happy until Cassiopea had returned from the dead past.

She had misjudged Cassiopea. She was a grown woman now and she could understand a great deal more than when

Cassiopea had first entered her father's life. She knew that, in a very large sense, it was Cassiopea who had brought her father back from the abyss. Cassiopea and time had healed Cain's wound. She could not have done that. Sheba knew this and she understood it, but still she could do nothing about her feelings toward Cassiopea. If only Cassiopea had been different, if only she had been something less than what she was, it would have been a simple matter to detest her. Sheba would have felt justified in her feelings. But Cassiopea was a good woman. She had courage and selflessness, all the qualities Sheba admired.

"*Damn* it," Sheba swore in a half-whisper, "it's just not fair!"

"Stand by to launch," said Tolen.

"Well, you've done it this time, Starbuck old chum," the pilot said to himself. "This time you really got in over your head. Three-to-one odds. Not good. Could be worse, but still not good. Anyone with any sense would simply fold. Anyone but Starbuck, that is. No, Starbuck always toughs it out. Starbuck always bluffs his way through somehow. Here he is, the Viper ace, sitting in his cockpit and waiting to be launched into action. Waiting to power out there on full thrusters and meet the dreaded Cylon armada; waiting to single-handedly dive into a cloud of fighters, biting, clawing, kicking and scratching his way into immortality with lasers blazing, waiting to see if this blind panic he's feeling will go away so he could stop talking to himself already...."

"Stand by to launch," said Tolen.

"Oh, shit," said Starbuck.

"Launch!"

Starbuck was slammed back against his cockpit as his Viper hurtled down the launch tube.

"Shiiiiiiiiiiiiiiiiiiiiit!"

"Starbuck! Are you all right?" Apollo's voice came over his comcircuit as they left the launch tubes and started to form up.

Starbuck realized that he had inadvertently chinned on his comcircuit as they launched.

"Yeah, yeah, I'm fine. I just said this is it."

"It sounded more like—"

"Never mind what it sounded like, just fly, willya? I got enough to worry about without you droning in my ear."

Apollo smiled and shook his head. Starbuck was all right.

"Fighters launched and taking up a spearhead in front of the *Pegasus*," Tolen said.

"Enemy in range," said Sheba.

"Okay, baby," Cain replied, "it's up to you. Clear me a way right through 'em."

"You got it, Commander."

The Cylon squadron commander could not believe what he was seeing. One lone battlestar against three base ships and all their squadrons. The humans must have lost their minds.

"They are heading directly for us," the Cylon squadron leader said. "Prepare to engage."

"Commence firing," said Apollo.

The Vipers cut loose with their laser batteries the moment they were within range. The Cylon fighters returned their fire and the space between them as they closed rapidly became an intricate latticework of deadly light. There were casualties on both sides, and the Cylons flared off from the attack, allowing the Vipers a way right through them so that they could regroup and take them on their next pass.

"Regroup," the Cylon squadron leader ordered his pilots. "The fighters will return to defend the *Pegasus*."

"Our Vipers blew a nice clean corridor right down the middle of their forces," Tolen said, "but they're coming in on us from all sides. We're in for it."

"Maintain course," Cain said in an icy voice. "Straight ahead, full speed. We've got to stay behind our Vipers as they cut through the second wave."

The *Pegasus* powered her way through the Cylon fighter squadron, taking several hits as she plowed through the crazily spinning ships that converged around her.

"The battlestar is not stopping to engage us," one of the Cylon fighter pilots reported to his squadron leader.

"Fools. They'll be trapped between our first and second attack flights. Unless they hope to scatter our second formation and make a run for it. Pursue and destroy."

The Cylon fighters regrouped and pursued the *Pegasus* while their second wave engaged the Vipers. The human pilots kept up a steady stream of fire, barely giving their laser batteries time to recycle.

"Starbuck..."

"Yo," the pilot replied to Apollo's voice over his com-circuit.

"There are so many of 'em, you can't miss."

Starbuck smiled mirthlessly at Apollo's efforts to keep their spirits up.

"Yeah, but I just lost Bunker and Taggs," he said. "We're getting it from all sides. The laser fire's so thick you could walk on it."

Cain was all over the bridge, taking reports from damage control and manning scanners himself in an effort to locate the base ships that had launched the Cylon assault.

"Where are they...." He slammed his fist down onto the console. "The damn fighters are like flies out there, they're throwing off the readings...."

Time. Time was crucial. They had to make Baltar think they were attempting a diversion in order to buy time for the *Galactica* and for themselves.

"Sir," said Tolen from another console, "we've located them!"

Cain was at his side in an instant. "How close?"

"We can reach them within perhaps another hundred centons," Tolen replied.

Cain shook his head. "Too long. We've got to cut it closer. And I can't push this baby until Baltar's taken the bait."

"Suppose he doesn't?" Tolen said grimly. "He must know that Imperious Leader is no longer on Gomoray. Suppose he doesn't break off the assault and send his fighters on ahead? What then?"

"Going to be damned interesting, won't it?" said Cain.

"I'll say one thing, Commander," Tolen said, glancing from his screens to Cain and back again, "whatever happens, life aboard the *Pegasus* has never been boring."

Sheba's voice came on over the p.a. system.

"Silver Spar Squadron, regroup to protect the *Pegasus*," she said. "She's under heavy attack."

"Negative!" said Cain, bending forward quickly and speaking into his command console mike. "Belay that order! Squadrons are to continue straight ahead! Repeat, squadrons are to continue straight ahead!"

"If you don't get some protection," Sheba said, "you'll be trapped between their first and second attack waves!"

"We won't need protection if we keep on going," Cain said. "You have your orders."

"Yes, sir."

The first attack wave of Cylon fighter craft had regrouped and caught up to them, and the *Pegasus* came under heavy fire. One of the fighters scored a direct hit on the external scanner turrets as it made its pass. The turret was knocked out and the power flowed back along the lines as the system overloaded. Tolen was sitting at his console when the screen went crazy, and before he had time to so much as take a breath, the power surged through the console and it exploded in a shower of sparks, throwing him clear across the bridge.

"Tolen!" Cain ran to his side. Tolen was motionless. "Get me to the life station! We've got a casualty on the bridge!"

Starbuck reversed on the Cylon craft pursuing him and blew it into fragments. He quickly looked back over his shoulder.

"Apollo! *Pegasus* is taking heavy fire. . . . We can't keep on going, we've got to go back and help Cain."

"But Cain's orders were to punch a hole through the second wave so that he could bring the *Pegasus* through after us."

"Dammit, there isn't going to *be* a *Pegasus!* The Cylons are swarming all over her!"

"You're right," Apollo replied, having seen for himself Cain's desperate plight. "Let's go."

Their Vipers left the spearhead formation and turned to head back for the *Pegasus*. As they were pulling out of the formation, Sheba, who was spearheading the squadrons, took a direct hit, even as the Silver Spar group broke through the second wave of Cylon fighters.

"Sheba! Are you all right?" Apollo said. Her Viper was moving very erratically.

"I don't think so," she replied, her pain evident in her voice.

"Can you control your Viper?"

"Uhhh. . . . Just barely. My guidance system is shot up. I can't fire, lasers won't respond. . . ."

"Okay, I'll move in front of you.... Try to follow me in. We're going to make a try for the Beta landing bay on the *Pegasus*."

"Thanks, Apollo...."

Starbuck moved in to cover Sheba from the rear. The second Cylon attack-wave formation had been broken up, but they were regrouping even as the *Pegasus* closed with them, trying to follow on the heels of the Viper squadrons before the Cylons could regroup and cut her off. The first Cylon attack wave was in pursuit, its lead ships making passes over the battlestar and trying to walk their fire into the bridge.

"I just hope the *Pegasus* is still around when we get there," Starbuck said.

The Cylon squadron leader in charge of the first wave communicated with Lucifer, aboard Baltar's ship. Lucifer received the message and hurried to relay it to Baltar.

"Baltar, another report—"

"Excellent! The *Pegasus* is destroyed and our forces are on their way to Gomoray to take care of Adama once and for all," said Baltar, with a vulpine grin on his face.

"Not exactly," Lucifer replied.

"What do you mean, not exactly?" Baltar snapped. "What's happened?"

"The battlestar and her warriors are not stopping to engage our fighters. The first-wave squadron leader reports that the Vipers broke through their formation and that the *Pegasus* followed in the wake of their spearhead. The Vipers have now contacted the second attack wave and it seems they are following a similar strategy."

Baltar frowned. "They're not engaging? But that's impossible, surely they were sent to stop our..." His voice trailed off. "Of course! Why didn't I see it before?"

"See what, sir?"

"Now it makes perfect sense," said Baltar. "They are a decoy. They're attempting hit and run tactics, trying to break through our formations in order to lead our fighters off, make them pursue and burn off fuel while Gomoray remains under attack!"

"A very clever plan," said Lucifer.

"Yes, but I see right through it," Baltar said with glee. His face was smug with self-satisfaction. "It's not going to work. Break off the attack. Order our fighters to continue on to Gomoray. We will finish off the *Galactica* and then return for the *Pegasus* after we've saved Imperious Leader."

The second Cylon attack wave began to converge upon the *Pegasus,* joining the first wave, which had already closed with the battlestar as it sought to follow full speed in the wake of her Viper squadrons.

"We can now finish her off," said the second-wave commander to the leader of the first attack wave. At that moment, Lucifer's voice came over their comcircuits.

"Squadrons are to disengage at once and move with all dispatch to Gomoray, repeat, squadrons are to disengage at once and continue to Gomoray."

"But we can destroy the *Pegasus* . . ."

"You have your orders," Lucifer said.

Both attack waves veered off from the *Pegasus,* reformed and continued on course to Gomoray.

"Boomer!" said Starbuck.

"I see it," Boomer replied, "but I don't believe it!"

"He was right," said Starbuck. "By Kobol, Cain was right again! They took the bait!"

"Say again?"

"Later. Let's get aboard and see how bad off the *Pegasus* is."

As they approached the battlestar, they could see that the Cylons would have finished her had they not broken off their assault. Cain might have minimized the damage he had taken by flying evasive tactics, but he had continued dead on course, doing what he could to fight off the Cylons with his laser batteries. As they landed and left their fighters, they could see that the damage control teams were working overtime. Several electrical fires had broken out in the landing bay and smoke was everywhere. Three of the external scanner turrets had been knocked out and the *Pegasus* had lost one of her aft laser batteries. There was no telling what other damage had been caused to her hull and circuits. Cain had survived yet another firefight, but only barely. If the Cylon squadrons hadn't taken his gambit and broken off their assault, nothing could have saved the ship. If Baltar had delayed in ordering them to break off their assault, the *Pegasus* would have been destroyed. Cain had cut it awfully close and it was fortunate that Baltar must not have known just how badly off the battlestar was.

Cassiopea was exhausted. There were a lot of wounded. She was bending over Tolen as Cain entered the life station.

"How is he?" Cain said with concern.

"He's taken a pretty heavy shock," she replied. "Burns, broken ribs he must have sustained when he was thrown clear of the console. There's some internal hemorrhaging—"

"Dammit, Cassi, is he going to live?"

"He'll live. I'm not so sure about many of the others."

They were bringing in even more wounded. They were getting first priority. There had not been time to ascertain the death toll. There was no point in counting; her concern was with the living, keeping them alive.

"We paid a high price," she said as she worked to stop

Tolen's bleeding. "Did we win?"

"Nobody ever wins," said Cain.

"It's taken you a long time to find that out."

"No. You were around me only for the parlor games. This is the real thing."

"You couldn't stand losing parlor games, either," Cassiopea said. "It just wasn't as painful to the people around you."

"Cassi..." His voice was strained. "What would you have had me do?"

She never had a chance to answer him. Apollo and Starbuck rushed into the life station with a gurney accompanied by a med tech. Sheba was lying on the gurney.

"Sheba..." said Cassiopea.

Cain rushed to his daughter's side. "Baby, are you all right?"

She smiled weakly. "Sorry, Father. I missed one."

Cain looked desperately at the tech. "What happened? How is she?"

"If you'll move out of the way, Commander," said Cassiopea, "we'll see what we can do."

They quickly moved the gurney over to one of the support cylinders and placed Sheba inside.

"What happened?" Cain demanded of Starbuck and Apollo. "How was she hurt?"

"I wish I could tell you that everything's just fine," Apollo said, "but I just don't know. They were all over us. I'm a pilot, not a med tech. She's in their hands now."

"What about the *Pegasus?*" said Starbuck. "Half the ship seems to be on fire."

"The damage isn't that bad and there'll be no more fighter assaults if you carry out my orders. As soon as it's physically possible," said Cain, "I want all of the wounded and nonessential personnel shuttled off to the fleet. You'll fly a fighter escort."

"What about the rest of the people on the *Pegasus?*" Apollo said. "What about you? What are you up to, Commander?"

"I don't have time to explain that now. But if you want to see these people survive, you'll get going. I want them off this ship in twenty centons."

He moved toward Cassiopea.

"Can she be moved?" he asked, indicating Sheba.

"Soon as I've got her out of triage," she replied. "But moved where?"

"Apollo and Starbuck will explain. The lives of all these people are in their hands. I've got work to do."

He pivoted and hurried out of the life station.

"Is he thinking of doing what I think he's thinking of doing?" said Starbuck, looking after him.

"Yeah," Apollo nodded. "And you know what bothers me the most? We're both starting to think like him."

"What is it?" said Cassiopea. "What's going on?"

"Just get your wounded ready to travel," said Apollo. "And make it fast."

CHAPTER THIRTEEN

Adama paced nervously on the bridge of the *Galactica*. At that very moment, he thought, Cain was flying into Hell. If he could only succeed in decoying the attack force away from them without getting caught himself. . . .

"The ground crews report that fuel loading is almost complete," said Colonel Tigh, moving up to his side. "We've already taken on more fuel than we could have hoped for. That Cylon depot's going to be dry after this last run."

"Sir," said Athena, "scanners are picking up a large body of incoming ships, unmistakably Cylon fighters."

Tigh and Adama exchanged quick glances.

"It looks like Cain's plan didn't work," he said. "He wasn't able to lead them off. Or there were just too many of them and . . ."

"Sir, there are many possibilities," said Tigh.

"And probabilities?"

Tigh shook his head. "I don't know. But we can't leave those fuel tankers on the ground. Fully loaded, they're not going to be able to move very fast. They'll be sitting targets."

Adama nodded grimly. "Notify the ground teams to close down and make ready to launch. Get those fuel tankers airborne, then have the shuttles pull the troops in."

He turned to Athena.

"How long do we have until the Cylon fighters intercept us?"

"Twenty centons and closing," she said.

Adama shook his head. "We'll never make it. It finally looks like we've just plain run out of time. And luck. Lord help us. If Cain hasn't gotten himself killed, perhaps he can get back to us in time to—" Adama shook his head. In time to do what? Still, he was their only chance. If he was still alive. "Athena, see if you can get me a long-range scanner reading on the *Pegasus*." *If it's still out there,* he thought.

Athena switched to long-range scanners. Adama waited tensely. Finally she looked up with a puzzled expression.

"Telemetry coming through is confusing, sir. According to the readings, the *Pegasus* is on a direct course toward the Cylon base ships. But . . . that can't be."

Tigh checked her readings. "He must have resumed a course toward them when he was unsuccessful in leading their fighters away."

"If he ever attempted to lead them away," said Adama tersely.

"But that was the plan," said Tigh.

"No, Tigh," Adama replied, "that was *our* plan. It was never his. The fool. Athena, priority communication on scramble, get me Commander Cain."

"Yes, sir . . . coming through. . . ."

Cain's face appeared on the monitor screen. He looked haggard.

"You're looking well, Adama," he said jauntily. "I trust the skies over Gomoray will remain clear for some time yet."

"Cain! What is your present course?"

Cain grinned. "You wouldn't be asking me that if you didn't already know."

Adama clenched his fists. "I order you to change course at once. We've got incoming Cylon fighters on our scanners and you're steering directly into those base ships. You'll kill every man and woman aboard the *Pegasus!*"

"Commander. . . . I have already made arrangements to dispatch all wounded and nonessential personnel to the fleet. They should already be arriving as you get back from Gomoray."

"Cain, you and I had an agreement. You were *not* to jeopardize lives needlessly. I—"

"Adama, we see things differently," Cain interrupted him. "I think I can promise you that you won't have to shoot your way out of Gomoray's atmosphere. You and the fleet will be safe."

"And what about you and your crew?"

"If my plan works," said Cain, "those ships your scanners are picking up will shortly turn around and come back my way. By the time they get here, there may not be a place for them to land. They'll drift forever in fuelless coffins."

"Cain! By all that's holy, will you *listen* to me?" said Adama desperately. "You can accomplish the same thing by veering away from those base ships at the last micron. Don't attempt to take them on!"

The commander of the *Pegasus* shook his head.

"Then their fighters will be able to refuel and go after you and your fleet," he said. "No, Adama. There is no choice. At the very least, I have to get rid of one or two of their base ships to prevent them from overwhelming you."

"You realize that I could relieve you of your command," Adama said, playing his last card.

"Adama, I beg of you," said Cain, "don't make my last battle an act of mutiny. Send me in with your blessing."

Adama sighed. There was nothing he could do, nothing he could say. Cain was determined to live up to his nickname of the Juggernaut. He would not be deterred from his course.

"I cannot give you my blessing, Cain," Adama said. "But I send my prayers to you and to each member of your crew."

"Thank you, Adama." He smiled weakly. "And, perhaps for the final time, Cain out."

The screen went blank.

Baltar waited impatiently for reports from his attack squadrons. By this time they should have come within range of their target. Things could not have worked out better for him. He would catch them with forces on the ground, with their fleet undefended and nothing Adama could do would enable him to escape. A human victory, even a temporary one such as they had achieved the last time, was completely out of the question. Their pathetic ploy had not worked. He had not been fooled by their transparent attempt to decoy his forces away from Gomoray. Their gambit had failed and as a result their strength was halved. The humans had doomed themselves.

Baltar suddenly caught himself. A *human* victory was out of the question, he had thought. The *humans* had doomed themselves. But he was human, too. Was he already thinking of himself as being Cylon?

Baltar smiled. Well, after all, why not? Had they not destroyed the colonies with *his* help? Could they have so successfully managed to deceive the Council without *his* efforts on their behalf? And had he not been rescued from death when they recognized his true worth to them, to be given a force comprised of three base ships? Had not the responsibility of hunting down the *Galactica* and her fleet been entrusted to *him?* What else did that make him if not a Cylon? Imperious Leader had even given him Lucifer, the most sophisticated of the I.L. series, as his second-in-command. He had even allowed him to design a throne room aboard his ship just like the one Imperious Leader himself had on his flagship. Was not that ample proof of his standing with the Cylons?

This day, thought Baltar, will mark the end for Adama and for the *Galactica.* It will mark the end for the human fleet, for the *Pegasus,* and a new beginning for himself. He would be welcomed on the surface of Gomoray as a savior, no doubt by Imperious Leader himself. He could expect a richly deserved reward. What should he ask for from the most powerful race in all the universe? The governorship of a planet? A kingdom of his own, his own pocket empire? Perhaps they would give him Gomoray.

Yes, he would ask for Gomoray. Why should they refuse him, the man who had saved a world that was a center of Cylon culture, the man who saved the life of the supreme Cylon himself? Gomoray would be perfect. He would be able to rule from his seat in the capital, with its graceful crystalline architecture. He would be able to import whatever he desired to live in luxury for the rest of—

"I bring news," said Lucifer, gliding into the room.

Baltar had never been able to get used to the silence with which the I.L. series Cylon moved. If he hadn't seen his approach, the sound of his surreal voice beside him always made him jump a little. He suspected that Lucifer enjoyed it.

"Our forces should be just about to Gomoray, where they will annihilate Adama," Baltar said, annoyed at having had his reverie disturbed.

"It is the *Pegasus* I am concerned about," said Lucifer.

Baltar made a gesture of dismissal.

"The *Pegasus* was nothing but a decoy. A pathetic effort to lead us off across the stars while the fleet escaped."

"But the *Pegasus* did not head off across the stars," said Lucifer.

"Oh?" Baltar raised his eyebrows. "Ah, yes, of course. When they discovered that their plan failed, the *Pegasus* turned around in a vain attempt to get back to Gomoray in time to save the *Galactica*. As if there would be anything that they could do, even if they were to arrive in time. No matter. She will not be able to beat our fighters to Gomoray."

"No, sir," said Lucifer, "because the *Pegasus* did not head back toward Gomoray either."

"Lucifer, would you come to the point? If the *Pegasus* did not head back toward Gomoray or go off away from us, then where *is* she heading?"

"Directly toward *us*, sir."

Baltar stared at Lucifer in astonishment.

"Directly toward *us?* But...but that's absurd! He is allowing us to destroy the *Galactica*, to wipe out the fleet.... Who in his right mind would do that?"

"May I suggest the legendary Commander Cain?" said Lucifer.

"Cain! Yes, Cain, of course. That would be just like

him. The man's insane. Once the Juggernaut makes up his mind to do something. . . . What does he care of the fleet or the *Galactica?* He wants. . ."

Baltar's voice dropped to a whisper.

"My God!" He turned pale. "He wants *me!* And he's just crazy enough to attack three base ships all by himself. But he must realize he has no chance. We outnumber him three to one, and our fighters. . . . Our fighters! Lucifer, recall our fighter squadron at once!"

Panic-stricken, Baltar ordered the commanders of his two supporting base ships to take up position in front of him, while his own base ship fell back. Just in case the fighter squadrons didn't make it back in time before Cain intercepted him, he wanted as much firepower as possible between himself and the Juggernaut.

Colonel Tigh was amazed. "Sir, the incoming Cylon fighter squadrons have suddenly turned around and headed back the other way! It doesn't make any sense!"

"Yes, it makes perfect sense," Adama said. "Baltar has recalled them to save his own skin, just as Cain knew he would."

"You don't mean the *Pegasus*. . . . You mean he's *actually attacking* those three base ships? All on his own?"

Adama gritted his teeth. "That's exactly what he's doing. He's saved our lives. And at the expense of his own. *Damn you, Cain.*"

Apollo and Starbuck were about to climb aboard the Vipers when Cain approached them.

"Apollo . . . Starbuck. . . ."

"Sir?"

"I just want you to know that I think you're two of the finest warriors I've ever met," said Cain. "I can't think of anyone else I'd sooner trust with the lives of so many of my people."

"Between your squadrons and ours," said Apollo, "we'll get them to safety."

"Sir," said Starbuck.

"Yes, Starbuck, what is it?"

Starbuck hesitated. "There are those of us who . . . don't have a lot of attachments. . . . At least I don't. . . . I wouldn't mind seeing this one through with you to the end."

Cain smiled and clapped the pilot on the shoulder.

"Starbuck, I appreciate your offer. But if I'm right, a lot of Baltar's fighters will be turning around and heading right back this way to save Baltar's hide for him. Apollo will need every one of you to protect the shuttles on their way back to the fleet."

"But what about you?" said Starbuck. "Without fighters—"

"The Cylon base ships don't have any fighters right now, either," Cain said.

"But they have weaponry," Apollo said.

Cain nodded. "So does the *Pegasus*. We may be a bit shot up, but we can still fight. Besides, there's only one base ship I'm really interested in. Baltar's."

Apollo offered him his hand. "Good luck."

"You, too."

"That goes double for me, sir," Starbuck said.

Cain shook both their hands and moved away, walking quickly without looking back.

"Why do I have the feeling I won't be seeing him again?" said Starbuck.

"I don't know, Starbuck," said Apollo. "I don't have that feeling. And I can't tell you why, because when you consider the odds, there's no way he can survive. But then, that's the story of his whole career, isn't it?"

They climbed aboard their ships.

Cain waited at the elevator, personally seeing off each of his wounded crew. Many of them were incapable of seeing him, but he was there to see them off, just the same. The nonessential personnel had already boarded the shuttles. Cassiopea came out of the elevator with a med tech and a gurney bearing Sheba.

"Father," she said, reaching out a hand to him, "I don't want to go."

Cain gently stroked her hair, then bent down and kissed her.

"Better hurry with this one, Cassi," he said. "The other shuttles are all loaded and ready to launch."

"I guess you two would like a private moment to say goodbye," said Sheba.

Cassiopea shook her head. "No, there's nothing I could or ever have said to your father that I wouldn't be proud to say in front of you, Sheba."

She moved up close to Cain and placed her fingertips lightly on his cheek.

"You're a very special man," she said. She smiled. "A hard man, but a special man. Whatever happens, I want you to know that I'm glad to have been a small part of your life. And I'll never forget you, you old wardaggit."

She kissed him. The final countdown to launch began. Cain glanced down at Sheba and smiled.

"Goodbye, baby."

"I'll see you soon," she said, but her voice caught.

"You bet."

Cain hurried to the bridge and stopped the moment he entered, stunned. Tolen was propped up at his station behind the console. His chest was in a plastic support harness and his hands were bandaged.

"What the hell are *you* doing here?" Cain demanded.

"All wounded personnel are supposed to be—"

"Forget it, Commander," Tolen said. "I'm sticking."

"You realize this is insubordination," Cain said.

"Yeah. So court-martial me." Tolen laughed, grimacing in pain.

Cain laughed with him. "Damn you, Tolen, if we get through this, I'll kick your butt up between your shoulders."

"*If* we get through this?" Tolen said. "You lunatic, what makes you think we've even got a chance?"

Both men were silent for a long moment.

"It's been a long haul, hasn't it?" said Cain.

Tolen nodded. "Yeah. And it's been a good one. Damn. Wish we had time for a drink."

"Tell me about it. When this is over, I'm buying."

Tolen shook his head and grinned ruefully. "Sure." He thumbed on his mike. "Launch shuttles. And fighter protection." He thumbed off the mike and shrugged. "What the hell, why take them with us?"

"Range to base ships?" said Cain.

"Thirty centons. And closing," said Tolen. He checked his console. "All ships launched and under way."

"Right," said Cain, "let's do it. We've got a very important appointment with a man named Baltar."

Baltar fidgeted on his throne, chewing on his lower lip.

"How long before our fighters can return to defend us?" he asked Lucifer nervously.

"I'm afraid the *Pegasus* will reach us first," Lucifer replied.

Baltar wrung his hands. "Drop back still further and order the support ships to intercept the *Pegasus.*"

"I'm not sure the other base ship commanders will appreciate that," said Lucifer.

"Damn you, Lucifer, it isn't a request! It's an order!"

"As you command, sir."

Tolen shifted slightly in his chair, wincing with pain. He moistened his lips.

"Two base ships coming up on range," he said. "The third has fallen back behind them."

"That'll be Baltar's ship," said Cain. "How obliging of him to let us know which ship he's on. Plot a course between the two base ships. Arm all missiles and bring defense shields to maximum power."

Starbuck watched his scanner and made several quick calculations. Then he smiled and chinned on his comcircuit.

"Apollo...."

"Go ahead, Starbuck."

"According to my scanner and some calculations I've just made, our vector to the fleet will take these shuttles well out of the path of those returning Cylon fighter squadrons."

"That was the whole idea," Apollo replied. "We don't want to lead them back to a fleet of defenseless civilian ships."

"Sure," said Starbuck, "and that means they don't really need our protection. I mean, those fighters aren't coming after us, they're going to return to the base ships before they do anything else, right? And what's one less Viper...or two, if you get my meaning?"

"I get it," said Apollo. "But what you're talking about is violating orders."

"Whose?"

"What do you mean, whose? Cain's."

"Now, how can we be accused of violating orders of a

man who isn't following orders himself?" said Starbuck.

"Somehow that makes sense," Apollo said.

"Are you with me?"

"Boomer," said Apollo.

"Yo. . . ."

"You're in command," Apollo said. "Starbuck and I want to check out our rear flank."

"Rear flank, huh?" said Boomer. "How far to our rear?"

"Don't ask too many questions," said Apollo.

"That's what I thought," Boomer replied. "You guys are crazy. But good luck."

Starbuck's and Apollo's Vipers peeled off from the formation and turned back, under full power, toward the *Pegasus*.

Tolen checked his screens, did a double take, then checked them again.

"Commander?"

"Are we in missile range?" said Cain tensely.

"Coming up on it," Tolen replied, "but there're two Vipers approaching us at just sub-light speed."

"What? Who is it? What the hell are they up to? Identify . . ."

"No time, sir. Target range, two base ships dead ahead. . . ."

The two base ships opened up with their forward laser batteries.

"Negative shield," said Cain. The shield slid down over the bridge observation port and they were now dependent entirely upon their instruments, with several scanner turrets not functioning. "Return fire," said Cain.

Apollo's hands tensed on the controls of his Viper.

"There they are," he said. "Looks like he intends to try and go between them."

"Let's see if we can't knock out their flank missile launchers," Starbuck said.

"Oh, boy. Well, who wants to live forever? I'll take the ship on the right," Apollo said.

"I'll get the other one...."

With engines working to the limit, both pilots went in under full thrusters, diving down and passing over the *Pegasus* as they swooped down upon the base ships, darting from side to side to avoid laser fire.

"Sir!" said Tolen. "Those two Vipers are attempting a strafing run on those base ships dead ahead!"

Cain sat up straight, leaning forward, his hands grasping the arms of his chair tightly.

"Starbuck and Apollo!" he exclaimed. "I *told* them..."

"They seem to be angling for the flankside missile launchers on both ships," said Tolen.

"They're clearing a way through for us," said Cain. He smashed his fist down on the console. "Come on, boys, go! *Go!*"

Apollo streaked in with Starbuck on his flank. The base ships loomed impossibly large before them, looking like small planets. They could both see the forward batteries as they swiveled to aim at them, and almost at the same time both Vipers rolled, diving in between the two base ships.

Apollo looked "up" to see the massive hull of the base ship directly "overhead." For a moment he had the illusion that the gargantuan craft was falling down on him, about to squash him like a bug, but it quickly passed as he oriented himself to the new perspective.

"You know, it's kind of nice in here," he said to Starbuck. "They can't fire at us without hitting each other."

"Trouble is, we can't stay in here," Starbuck replied. "We'd better make it count."

"Right. Let's give it to them!"

Both Vipers cut loose, blasting with their lasers, raking the sides of the base ships, pausing only to allow their lasers to recycle before they fired again. Then they were through, hurtling away from both ships and rolling, flying evasive maneuvers.

"Scanners report solid damage to both base ships," Tolen said excitedly, "here . . . here, and here!"

He pointed on the large screen showing the base ships, indicating where Starbuck and Apollo had scored very telling hits.

"I'll be damned," said Cain. "They did it! That's what I call flying!"

"And shooting," Tolen said.

"All right, let's not let 'em down. We're going in. Arm missiles for point-blank range. Even their shields won't be able to help them."

Amid a veritable sea of energy beams, the three ships came together like huge mechanized titans clashing to slug it out.

"Closing to blank range," said Tolen, jerking briefly as a shower of sparks fell on him from an exploding monitor screen overhead. "Ten . . . nine. . . ."

"Starbuck!" said Apollo. "My scanner shows incoming Cylons, must be a thousand of 'em!"

"Give or take a few hundred, huh?" said Starbuck. He was flying more than his Viper. He was soaring on the most incredible adrenaline high his body had ever experienced. The sheer terror of diving down between those two base ships had triggered off a surge of indescribable vitality within him. "We can't leave now," said Starbuck, "I want to see what happens. And we still have to get that third base ship."

"Starbuck, for God's sake," Apollo said, "we can't fight off several Cylon fighter squadrons!"

"Apollo . . . we've come this far. . . ."

"Right, and I'm not about to end the journey here," Apollo said.

"But we—"

"Starbuck! Snap out of it! Negative, you understand me? No way! We've done all we can!"

"Three . . . two . . . one," said Tolen."

"Fire missiles!" Cain said.

At the last possible moment, Cain rolled the *Pegasus*, dodging the fire from the base ships' forward batteries, and the battlestar hurtled between the two Cylon craft at an incredible speed with missiles firing, slamming into the base ships.

Apollo looked back to see an impossibly bright wash of light against the velvet dark of space.

"Did you see that?" Starbuck shouted.

"I can't see a thing but spots," Apollo replied. "I've never seen a flash like that."

"Can you see the Pegasus?"

"No, I can't tell if he made it or not."

"What do we do?"

The Cylon fighter squadrons were closing fast.

"We get the hell out of here," Apollo said, "and go home—as fast as we can!"

The *Galactica* was under way, the fuel having been distributed throughout the fleet. When Starbuck and Apollo rendezvoused with the battlestar, Adama had been overjoyed, although he tried to hide his feelings behind a stoic exterior. He had never expected to see either one of them again.

That's twice I've lost them, Adama thought, only to have them restored to me again. Although he would never allow Starbuck to know it, Adama felt about him as though he were an adopted son. In a way, he was. Flamboyant, insubordinate, a maverick, but still, a son. As different from his true son, Apollo, as it was possible to be, yet still they were like brothers.

It seemed to Adama that an entire lifetime had passed since they had gone out on patrol together and failed to return. He thought he had lost them then, but they had returned, bringing with them another man Adama had thought long dead.

Cain. What could anybody make of Cain? They called him the "living legend," the Juggernaut, a name he richly deserved, for he was as stubborn and implacable as any man Adama had ever met. They had been friends for years, for longer than their children were alive, although they had never spent a great deal of time together. Fate always took them down different paths. In many ways, they were like Starbuck and Apollo. Adama would look at Starbuck and see a budding Cain, brash, aggressive, certain of himself and self-centered, a man who could be easily disliked if it were not for compensating charms and irrefutable evidence of his abilities that justified his intensity and self-confidence. Apollo, on the other hand, was like his father. Cool, steady, compassionate, a man who hid his vulnerabilities beneath an exterior of military discipline. But at least Starbuck and Apollo were together. For all their quarrels, for all their disagreements and impatience with each other, Adama and Cain had been as close as it was possible for two men to be. Fate had brought them back together again and had again torn them apart. This time, forever, thought Adama.

As soon as the Vipers carrying Starbuck and Apollo were

aboard, Adama leaned back in his chair and closed his eyes, allowing himself to relax for the first time since it all began. The first time his prodigal sons had returned, they came back with Cain and he had saved their lives, the lives of every man and woman in the fleet. Moreover, he had done it *his* way, as he always had. It was an old joke that they used to have between them, that there were three ways to get anything done... the right way, the wrong way and Cain's way, but whether it was right or wrong, Cain's way always brought results. Well, now Starbuck and Apollo had returned from the dead a second time. Only this time, they came back alone.

Adama rose to his feet and took a deep breath. "I'll be in the life station," he told Athena.

She smiled and nodded. She knew how he had been feeling. Apollo was his favorite, although her father did not consciously act as though he were, and she understood. She did not resent her brother, rather she felt sorry that the strength of emotion between her father and her brother could not be brought out into the open. For reasons of their own, owing to the nature of their personalities, father and son could never really show the love they felt for one another. They hid behind their roles as Captain and Commander, but the love was there, nevertheless. Both men knew it though, like many men, they had difficulty in finding ways to express it.

There were many times when she wished that she could be out there in a Viper, flying with her brother's squadron, but she knew that every time Apollo departed on a mission, part of Adama's heart went with him. She could only imagine how her father felt at such times. There was the fact that she was the most qualified person aboard to do her job, and the fact that, besides Starbuck, Apollo was the finest pilot in the fleet, better than she could ever hope to be. Yet she also understood that it was necessary for Adama to keep her by his side. He needed to know that she was there. Like Cain, Adama, too, had lost his wife. Unlike Cain, he had an incredible weight of responsibility for all the people in the fleet. Unlike Cain, he never had someone like Cassiopea to help him through the hard times. All he had was the *Galactica*. Thanks to Cain, the *Galactica* had once again been saved.

It's over, thought Athena as she watched her father leave the bridge. This time.

Cassiopea glanced up as Adama entered with Starbuck and Apollo. Sheba was lying down on one of the beds.

"Not too long," said Cassiopea. "She needs to build her strength back up."

Sheba squeezed Cassiopea's hand before she moved away.

"Any word?" Sheba asked anxiously.

"No," Adama said. He hesitated. "But that doesn't mean a thing. He wouldn't break communication silence and reveal his position."

Sheba gave him a small smile. She blinked back tears.

"Thanks for trying," she said, "but what are the odds against their surviving all those fighters? And that other base ship?" She shook her head.

"What were the odds when we thought you were all lost over two yahrens ago?" said Adama.

"Far as I'm concerned," said Starbuck, "he just headed out into deep space the way he did the last time. Those fighters couldn't have followed very far with empty fuel cells. They'd flown a long way already."

"In the meantime," said Adama, "until we hear from

your father, I want you to consider yourself a part of the family."

He took her hand and squeezed it.

"I already do," she said.

"I think you should let her rest now," said Cassiopea, ushering them out of the life station. At the door, Starbuck paused.

"Cassi, look . . ." He paused uncertainly. "I know things have been hard the last—"

She stopped him by putting a finger to his lips.

"Don't say it. Now is not the time or the place."

"Yes, but—"

"Why don't you come and see me later, in my cabin, when I've gone off duty? We can talk then, if you like. Or we don't have to talk."

She leaned forward and kissed him lingeringly on the lips. Then she went back into the life station, closing the doors behind her. Starbuck stood staring at the doors for a moment, then sighed and scratched his head.

"God damn. I need a drink." He moved off toward the Officers' Club.

Apollo and Adama walked slowly side by side down the corridor. For a while they didn't speak.

"It must be hard for her," Apollo said finally.

Adama nodded. "Yes."

"He was a hell of a man, wasn't he?"

"Yes. He was."

"I . . . I don't know what I'd do if I lost you," Apollo said.

Adama stopped. He swallowed heavily and turned to face his son. For a moment, both men simply stood there, staring at each other, then Adama stepped forward and put his arms around his son, crushing him to him in a strong embrace. Apollo hugged him back, but they broke apart when they saw several crew members approaching. They stood there briefly, feeling awkward and embarrassed, then Apollo said, "What do you say, Commander—want to go visit your adopted grandson?"

Adama smiled. "Yes, I do. Very much."

They walked off down the corridor together. They didn't even notice that they kept in step.

POUL ANDERSON

Masterpieces of Science Fiction

MS READ-a-thon—
a simple way to start youngsters reading

Boys and girls between 6 and 14 can join the MS READ-a-thon and help find a cure for Multiple Sclerosis by reading books. And they get two rewards — the enjoyment of reading, and the great feeling that comes from helping others.

Parents and educators: For complete information call your local MS chapter. Or mail the coupon below.

Kids can help, too!